SPECTRUM®

Subtraction

Grade 2

Published by Spectrum®
an imprint of Carson-Dellosa Publishing
Greensboro, NC

Spectrum®
An imprint of Carson-Dellosa Publishing LLC
P.O. Box 35665
Greensboro, NC 27425 USA

ISBN 978-1-4838-3108-4

01-053167784

Table of Contents Subtraction

Check What You Know

Subtraction Facts through 20

Subtract.

5 − 4	14 − 7	6 − 4	10 − 5	13 − 5	18 − 9
11 − 4	19 − 7	9 − 6	4 − 4	16 − 8	15 − 9
17 − 8	8 − 5	3 − 0	20 − 3	12 − 4	7 − 2
20 − 7	9 − 2	13 − 8	7 − 0	16 − 5	11 − 9
6 − 5	15 − 6	17 − 7	4 − 2	8 − 3	19 − 3
12 − 2	5 − 4	10 − 7	18 − 5	14 − 6	3 − 0

NAME _____

Check What You Know

SHOW YOUR WORK

Subtraction Facts through 20

Solve each problem.

The Jones family borrows 12 books from the library.

The Gomez family borrows 8 books.

How many more books does the Jones family borrow? _____

There are 17 slices of pizza.

8 of them get eaten.

How many slices are left? _____

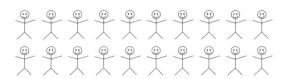

20 students are in the library.

6 students leave.

How many students are still in the library? _____

Sue borrows 12 books.

If Nina borrows 4 fewer books than Sue, how many books does Nina borrow? _____

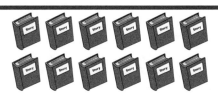

There are 18 desks on the first floor.

There are 7 desks on the second floor.

How many more desks are on the first floor? _____

Lesson 1.1 Subtracting from 0 through 5

There are 4 fish. 2 swim away.
How many fish are left?

$$\begin{array}{r} 4 \\ -2 \\ \hline 2 \end{array} \leftarrow \text{difference}$$

Subtract.

$$\begin{array}{r} 4 \\ -1 \\ \hline 3 \end{array} \qquad \begin{array}{r} 3 \\ -3 \\ \hline \end{array} \qquad \begin{array}{r} 1 \\ -1 \\ \hline \end{array} \qquad \begin{array}{r} 5 \\ -4 \\ \hline \end{array} \qquad \begin{array}{r} 3 \\ -0 \\ \hline \end{array} \qquad \begin{array}{r} 5 \\ -2 \\ \hline \end{array}$$

$$\begin{array}{r} 2 \\ -2 \\ \hline \end{array} \qquad \begin{array}{r} 1 \\ -0 \\ \hline \end{array} \qquad \begin{array}{r} 5 \\ -5 \\ \hline \end{array} \qquad \begin{array}{r} 4 \\ -3 \\ \hline \end{array} \qquad \begin{array}{r} 5 \\ -3 \\ \hline \end{array} \qquad \begin{array}{r} 4 \\ -0 \\ \hline \end{array}$$

$$\begin{array}{r} 2 \\ -1 \\ \hline \end{array} \qquad \begin{array}{r} 4 \\ -2 \\ \hline \end{array} \qquad \begin{array}{r} 2 \\ -0 \\ \hline \end{array} \qquad \begin{array}{r} 0 \\ -0 \\ \hline \end{array} \qquad \begin{array}{r} 3 \\ -1 \\ \hline \end{array} \qquad \begin{array}{r} 4 \\ -1 \\ \hline \end{array}$$

$$\begin{array}{r} 2 \\ -1 \\ \hline \end{array} \qquad \begin{array}{r} 5 \\ -0 \\ \hline \end{array} \qquad \begin{array}{r} 4 \\ -4 \\ \hline \end{array} \qquad \begin{array}{r} 5 \\ -2 \\ \hline \end{array} \qquad \begin{array}{r} 2 \\ -2 \\ \hline \end{array} \qquad \begin{array}{r} 3 \\ -3 \\ \hline \end{array}$$

$$\begin{array}{r} 3 \\ -2 \\ \hline \end{array} \qquad \begin{array}{r} 4 \\ -1 \\ \hline \end{array} \qquad \begin{array}{r} 5 \\ -4 \\ \hline \end{array} \qquad \begin{array}{r} 4 \\ -2 \\ \hline \end{array} \qquad \begin{array}{r} 3 \\ -0 \\ \hline \end{array} \qquad \begin{array}{r} 5 \\ -1 \\ \hline \end{array}$$

Lesson 1.2 Subtracting from 6, 7, and 8

There are 7 balls.

5 are baseballs.

How many are not baseballs?

$$\begin{array}{r} 7 \\ -5 \\ \hline 2 \end{array}$$

Subtract.

8 − 4	7 − 1	6 − 3	7 − 3	8 − 5	6 − 2
7 − 0	8 − 7	6 − 4	7 − 7	8 − 3	6 − 6
6 − 1	8 − 2	7 − 4	6 − 5	8 − 6	7 − 5
8 − 8	6 − 0	7 − 2	8 − 1	8 − 0	7 − 6
6 − 2	8 − 3	8 − 4	7 − 3	7 − 7	6 − 3

Lesson 1.3 Subtracting from 9 and 10

Dani has 10 postage stamps.    10

Felix has 6 postage stamps.   − 6

How many more stamps does Dani have?   4 ← difference

Subtract.

9 − 6	10 − 5	9 − 3	10 − 4	10 − 9	9 − 7
10 − 1	9 − 8	9 − 5	10 − 8	9 − 1	10 − 6
9 − 0	9 − 4	10 − 7	9 − 2	10 − 3	10 − 0
9 − 9	10 − 2	9 − 3	10 − 9	10 − 1	9 − 5
9 − 8	10 − 5	9 − 1	9 − 7	10 − 8	10 − 3

Lesson 1.4 Subtracting from 11, 12, and 13

13 = 1 ten 3 ones

 Cross out to solve.

$$\begin{array}{r} 13 \\ -5 \\ \hline 8 \end{array}$$

12 = 1 ten 2 ones

 Cross out to solve.

$$\begin{array}{r} 12 \\ -7 \\ \hline 5 \end{array}$$

Subtract.

12 − 4	11 − 9	13 − 9	12 − 5	13 − 4	11 − 6
11 − 8	13 − 6	13 − 8	12 − 3	11 − 5	12 − 6
13 − 4	11 − 7	12 − 9	12 − 4	13 − 7	11 − 3
12 − 5	13 − 5	12 − 8	11 − 5	11 − 4	13 − 9
11 − 2	13 − 6	11 − 8	12 − 3	12 − 7	11 − 6

Lesson 1.5 Subtracting from 14, 15, and 16

16 − 9 7	Think: 16 = 1 ten 6 ones	15 − 6 9	Cross out to solve. 15 = 1 ten 5 ones

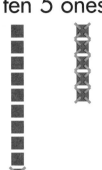

Subtract.

14 − 9	15 − 8	16 − 4	15 − 3	14 − 7	16 − 0

14 − 2	16 − 7	14 − 8	15 − 5	16 − 3	15 − 2

14 − 5	14 − 3	15 − 7	15 − 0	16 − 2	14 − 6

14 − 0	15 − 1	15 − 9	16 − 8	15 − 4	15 − 6

16 − 5	16 − 9	16 − 1	16 − 2	14 − 4	14 − 1

Lesson 1.6 Subtracting from 17, 18, 19, and 20

$$
\begin{array}{r}
17 \\
-\ 9 \\
\hline
8
\end{array}
$$

Subtract.

$\begin{array}{r}18\\-\ 9\\\hline\end{array}$	$\begin{array}{r}17\\-\ 3\\\hline\end{array}$	$\begin{array}{r}20\\-\ 6\\\hline\end{array}$	$\begin{array}{r}17\\-\ 9\\\hline\end{array}$	$\begin{array}{r}19\\-\ 5\\\hline\end{array}$	$\begin{array}{r}20\\-\ 9\\\hline\end{array}$
$\begin{array}{r}18\\-\ 8\\\hline\end{array}$	$\begin{array}{r}17\\-\ 8\\\hline\end{array}$	$\begin{array}{r}19\\-\ 1\\\hline\end{array}$	$\begin{array}{r}20\\-\ 8\\\hline\end{array}$	$\begin{array}{r}17\\-\ 7\\\hline\end{array}$	$\begin{array}{r}20\\-\ 3\\\hline\end{array}$
$\begin{array}{r}18\\-\ 7\\\hline\end{array}$	$\begin{array}{r}19\\-\ 9\\\hline\end{array}$	$\begin{array}{r}18\\-\ 4\\\hline\end{array}$	$\begin{array}{r}19\\-\ 7\\\hline\end{array}$	$\begin{array}{r}18\\-\ 6\\\hline\end{array}$	$\begin{array}{r}18\\-\ 2\\\hline\end{array}$
$\begin{array}{r}17\\-\ 4\\\hline\end{array}$	$\begin{array}{r}17\\-\ 5\\\hline\end{array}$	$\begin{array}{r}20\\-\ 7\\\hline\end{array}$	$\begin{array}{r}18\\-\ 3\\\hline\end{array}$	$\begin{array}{r}19\\-\ 3\\\hline\end{array}$	$\begin{array}{r}17\\-\ 2\\\hline\end{array}$
$\begin{array}{r}20\\-\ 5\\\hline\end{array}$	$\begin{array}{r}18\\-\ 1\\\hline\end{array}$	$\begin{array}{r}17\\-\ 6\\\hline\end{array}$	$\begin{array}{r}19\\-\ 8\\\hline\end{array}$	$\begin{array}{r}20\\-\ 2\\\hline\end{array}$	$\begin{array}{r}20\\-10\\\hline\end{array}$

Lesson 1.7 Subtraction Practice

Complete the subtraction table. Subtract each number at the top from each number along the side. When you finish, look at the numbers you wrote. What patterns do you notice?

−	1	2	3	4	5	6	7	8	9
20	19								
19									
18									
17				13					
16									
15									
14								6	
13									
12									
11									
10					5				
9									
8									
7			4						
6									
5					0				
4									
3									
2	1								
1									

Lesson 1.8 Problem Solving

Solve each problem.

Steve has 7 fish.

Ramon has 13 fish.

How many more fish does Ramon have? 6

$$\begin{array}{r} 13 \\ -7 \\ \hline 6 \end{array}$$

Yolanda has 14 teddy bears.

Maria has 6 teddy bears.

How many more does Yolanda have? _____

Gina bakes 15 cupcakes.

Her friends eat 7.

How many cupcakes are left? _____

6 students were in the classroom at 9:00.

19 students were in the classroom at 10:00.

How many students came in
between 9:00 and 10:00? _____

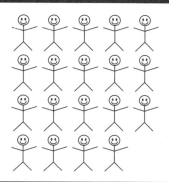

Mark has 18 toy cars.

He gives 9 away.

How many cars does he have left? _____

Lesson 1.8 Problem Solving

SHOW YOUR WORK

Solve each problem.

Yoko picks 12 flowers.

She gives 6 to her mother.

How many flowers does Yoko have now? _____

Taylor has 20 books.

5 of them are about sports.

How many of them are not about sports? _____

Jesse mows 19 lawns.

Martin mows 7 lawns.

How many more lawns does Jesse mow? _____

Together, Kiki and Sara have 9 books.

Kiki has 5 books.

How many books does Sara have? _____

$9 - 5 =$ _____

Check What You Learned

Subtraction Facts through 20

Subtract.

13 − 4	7 −1	4 −2	14 − 8	10 − 9	5 −0
19 − 9	15 − 6	6 − 6	17 − 8	8 −2	12 − 6
16 − 8	18 − 9	20 − 4	3 −3	11 − 8	9 −9
20 − 8	10 − 6	12 − 4	3 −1	16 − 9	7 −5
18 − 3	9 −2	11 − 7	15 − 9	6 −3	13 − 5
4 −0	14 − 5	2 −1	17 − 6	19 − 5	8 −4

Check What You Learned

Subtraction Facts through 20

Solve each problem.

There are 15 bananas.

Joe takes 6.

How many bananas are left? _____

The Changs picked 11 apples.

The next day, there were 3 apples left.

How many apples did the Changs eat? _____

The store has 12 boxes of plums.

5 boxes of plums are sold.

How many boxes are left? _____

Together, Grace and her sister bought 18 bananas.

Grace bought 9 bananas.

How many bananas did her sister buy? _____

$18 -$  $= 9$

Mrs. Lopez has 19 hats.

3 of the hats have bows.

How many hats do not have bows? _____

Check What You Know

Subtracting 2-Digit Numbers (No Renaming)

Subtract.

$$
\begin{array}{r} 46 \\ -41 \\ \hline \end{array}
\qquad
\begin{array}{r} 77 \\ -50 \\ \hline \end{array}
\qquad
\begin{array}{r} 63 \\ -43 \\ \hline \end{array}
\qquad
\begin{array}{r} 19 \\ -\ 6 \\ \hline \end{array}
\qquad
\begin{array}{r} 35 \\ -13 \\ \hline \end{array}
$$

$$
\begin{array}{r} 57 \\ -33 \\ \hline \end{array}
\qquad
\begin{array}{r} 88 \\ -61 \\ \hline \end{array}
\qquad
\begin{array}{r} 97 \\ -47 \\ \hline \end{array}
\qquad
\begin{array}{r} 29 \\ -12 \\ \hline \end{array}
\qquad
\begin{array}{r} 48 \\ -45 \\ \hline \end{array}
$$

$$
\begin{array}{r} 39 \\ -\ 4 \\ \hline \end{array}
\qquad
\begin{array}{r} 44 \\ -13 \\ \hline \end{array}
\qquad
\begin{array}{r} 67 \\ -61 \\ \hline \end{array}
\qquad
\begin{array}{r} 99 \\ -79 \\ \hline \end{array}
\qquad
\begin{array}{r} 54 \\ -32 \\ \hline \end{array}
$$

Solve each problem.

$46 -$ $=24$

Mara saw 46 . Then, some flew away.

Now, Mara sees only 24 .

How many flew away? _____

The store has 37 .

It has 25 . How many more

does it have than _____?

58 are on the field.

45 of the are playing soccer.

How many are not playing soccer? _____

Lesson 2.1 Subtracting 2-Digit Numbers

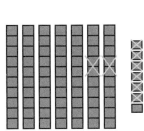

	First, subtract the ones.	Then, subtract the tens.

```
  77          77          77
- 26        - 26        - 26
              1          51
```

Subtract.

```
   49        87        36        54        68
 - 39      -  6      - 24      - 40      - 16
   10        81
```

```
   79        78        42        19        26
 - 63      - 25      - 12      -  7      - 11
```

```
   59        28        95        74        67
 - 38      - 14      - 62      - 50      - 41
```

```
   92        35        77        82        86
 - 81      -  5      - 17      - 51      - 64
```

```
   58        75        47        89        65
 - 53      - 61      - 37      - 27      - 60
```

Lesson 2.1 Subtracting 2-Digit Numbers

Subtract.

| 91 | 46 | 57 | 83 | 69 |
| − 80 | − 23 | − 32 | − 33 | − 55 |

| 34 | 48 | 73 | 56 | 76 |
| − 21 | − 22 | − 52 | − 23 | − 45 |

| 65 | 44 | 96 | 66 | 90 |
| − 13 | − 20 | − 85 | − 31 | − 70 |

| 43 | 72 | 88 | 94 | 29 |
| − 10 | − 30 | − 71 | − 84 | − 5 |

| 99 | 18 | 26 | 86 | 38 |
| − 8 | − 4 | − 22 | − 55 | − 27 |

| 78 | 93 | 59 | 82 | 77 |
| − 64 | − 3 | − 25 | − 50 | − 36 |

| 97 | 69 | 74 | 16 | 46 |
| − 72 | − 8 | − 12 | − 3 | − 35 |

Lesson 2.2 Subtraction Practice

Subtract. Use the tens blocks and ones blocks to help you.

$$\begin{array}{r} 66 \\ -\ 31 \\ \hline 35 \end{array}$$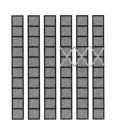

$$\begin{array}{r} 47 \\ -\ 16 \\ \hline \end{array}$$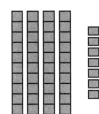

$$\begin{array}{r} 78 \\ -\ 27 \\ \hline \end{array}$$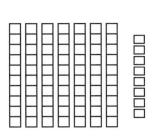

$$\begin{array}{r} 19 \\ -\ 12 \\ \hline \end{array}$$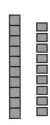

$$\begin{array}{r} 66 \\ -\ 26 \\ \hline \end{array}$$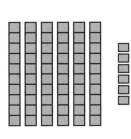

$$\begin{array}{r} 94 \\ -\ 30 \\ \hline \end{array}$$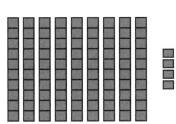

$$\begin{array}{r} 52 \\ -\ 11 \\ \hline \end{array}$$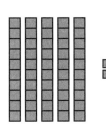

$$\begin{array}{r} 26 \\ -\ 13 \\ \hline \end{array}$$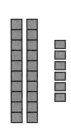

Lesson 2.2 Subtraction Practice

Subtract.

67 − 45	54 − 20	73 − 63	99 − 83	68 − 62
79 − 7	88 − 70	37 − 34	66 − 6	89 − 44
57 − 32	95 − 63	47 − 4	87 − 42	49 − 48
65 − 30	76 − 33	85 − 31	92 − 52	38 − 17
96 − 81	43 − 11	58 − 7	93 − 53	84 − 71
94 − 14	63 − 3	29 − 15	97 − 23	61 − 40
49 − 6	24 − 4	77 − 51	98 − 80	45 − 23

NAME _____

Lesson 2.3 Problem Solving

Solve each problem.

Ms. Willis has 28 .

She returns 10 .

How many does Ms. Willis have left? __18__

$$\begin{array}{r} 28 \\ -10 \\ \hline 18 \end{array}$$

The first-grade class has 32 .

The second-grade class has 30 .

How many more does the first-grade class have? _____

The art room has 65 .

Students are using 22 .

How many are not being used? _____

Students had 44 at breakfast.

They had 59 at lunch. How many

more did students have at lunch? _____

The library has 37 about computers. 37 − 12 = _____

12 of the have been borrowed. How

many about computers are still in the library? _____

Lesson 2.3 Problem Solving

Solve each problem.

Cara has 35 .

Ben has 39 .

How many more does Ben have? _____

Marcus has 48 .

He uses 30 to mail cards.

How many does he have left? _____

Pedro picks 39 .

Jessica picks 28 .

How many more did Pedro pick? _____

There are 29 students with or .

There are 9 students with .

How many students have ? _____

Toya picks 48 .

Jon picks 16 🍎.

How many more 🍎 than 🍎 do they have? _____

Check What You Learned

Subtracting 2-Digit Numbers (No Renaming)

Subtract.

79 − 63	44 − 20	68 − 55	52 − 11	85 − 35	26 − 4
99 − 46	76 − 6	19 − 16	45 − 12	76 − 42	39 − 15
77 − 4	64 − 54	95 − 70	37 − 7	29 − 12	96 − 52

CHAPTER 2 POSTTEST

Solve each problem.

Jermaine has 27 . Brian has 31 .

The boys lost 5 playing at the park.

How many total do they have now? _____

The class plants 35 .

The grow into 24 . 3 of the die.

How many does the class have? _____

Sydney makes 45 .

Rosa makes 65 .

How many more does Rosa make? _____

NAME _____

Check What You Know

Subtracting 2-Digit Numbers (With Renaming)

Subtract.

93	54	23	63	80
− 65	− 49	− 5	− 57	− 42

33	52	85	40	77
− 16	− 24	− 37	− 18	− 19

32	66	70	83	94
− 8	− 59	− 21	− 9	− 67

Solve each problem.

Anita picks 45 .

She picks 61 .

How many more than does she pick? _____

Max's bucket holds 72 .

Trey's bucket holds 44 .

How many more does Max's bucket hold? _____

Carol and Paula have 91 .

Paula picked 45 .

How many  did Carol pick? _____

91 − 45 = _____

Lesson 3.1 Subtracting 2-Digit Numbers

		Rename 1 ten as 10 ones.	Subtract the ones.	Subtract the tens.
33 −19 3 tens 3 ones = 2 tens 13 ones		$\overset{2\ 13}{\cancel{33}}$ −19	$\overset{2\ 13}{\cancel{33}}$ −19 4	$\overset{2\ 13}{\cancel{33}}$ −19 difference → 14
60 −28 6 tens 0 ones = 5 tens 10 ones		$\overset{5\ 10}{\cancel{60}}$ −28	$\overset{5\ 10}{\cancel{60}}$ −28 2	$\overset{5\ 10}{\cancel{60}}$ −28 difference → 32

Subtract.

$$
\begin{array}{r} \overset{2\ 16}{\cancel{36}} \\ -\ 7 \\ \hline 29 \end{array}
\qquad
\begin{array}{r} 51 \\ -39 \\ \hline \end{array}
\qquad
\begin{array}{r} 44 \\ -15 \\ \hline \end{array}
\qquad
\begin{array}{r} 84 \\ -47 \\ \hline \end{array}
\qquad
\begin{array}{r} 72 \\ -65 \\ \hline \end{array}
$$

$$
\begin{array}{r} 76 \\ -19 \\ \hline \end{array}
\qquad
\begin{array}{r} 90 \\ -78 \\ \hline \end{array}
\qquad
\begin{array}{r} 53 \\ -26 \\ \hline \end{array}
\qquad
\begin{array}{r} 94 \\ -85 \\ \hline \end{array}
\qquad
\begin{array}{r} 75 \\ -18 \\ \hline \end{array}
$$

$$
\begin{array}{r} 44 \\ -29 \\ \hline \end{array}
\qquad
\begin{array}{r} 83 \\ -46 \\ \hline \end{array}
\qquad
\begin{array}{r} 64 \\ -59 \\ \hline \end{array}
\qquad
\begin{array}{r} 50 \\ -29 \\ \hline \end{array}
\qquad
\begin{array}{r} 97 \\ -78 \\ \hline \end{array}
$$

$$
\begin{array}{r} 66 \\ -28 \\ \hline \end{array}
\qquad
\begin{array}{r} 32 \\ -17 \\ \hline \end{array}
\qquad
\begin{array}{r} 40 \\ -25 \\ \hline \end{array}
\qquad
\begin{array}{r} 57 \\ -29 \\ \hline \end{array}
\qquad
\begin{array}{r} 61 \\ -\ 5 \\ \hline \end{array}
$$

Lesson 3.1 Subtracting 2-Digit Numbers

	Rename 1 ten as 10 ones.	Subtract the ones.	Subtract the tens.
41 − 35	$\overset{3\ 11}{\cancel{4}\cancel{1}}$ − 35	$\overset{3\ 11}{\cancel{4}\cancel{1}}$ − 35 6	$\overset{3\ 11}{\cancel{4}\cancel{1}}$ − 35 difference → 6 Should you write a number in the tens place? _____

Subtract.

72 − 69 3	28 − 19	66 − 48	96 − 8	82 − 37
80 − 67	24 − 8	60 − 43	54 − 45	91 − 55
42 − 38	82 − 56	92 − 63	77 − 68	81 − 33
74 − 58	86 − 48	73 − 49	95 − 87	30 − 14
46 −27	31 − 23	71 − 34	22 − 6	96 − 69

Lesson 3.2 Subtraction Practice

Use the regrouped tens blocks and ones blocks to help you subtract. Rename each crossed-out digit by writing a number in the box above. Then, solve the problem.

2	16

$$\begin{array}{r} 2\!\!\!/6 \\ -\ 29 \\ \hline 7 \end{array}$$

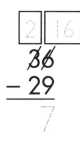

$$\begin{array}{r} \square\square \\ 8\!\!\!/1 \\ -\ 35 \\ \hline \end{array}$$

$$\begin{array}{r} \square\square \\ 4\!\!\!/4 \\ -\ 28 \\ \hline \end{array}$$

$$\begin{array}{r} \square\square \\ 7\!\!\!/8 \\ -\ 69 \\ \hline \end{array}$$

$$\begin{array}{r} \square\square \\ 5\!\!\!/3 \\ -\ 18 \\ \hline \end{array}$$

$$\begin{array}{r} \square\square \\ 6\!\!\!/5 \\ -\ 47 \\ \hline \end{array}$$

Lesson 3.2 Subtraction Practice

	Rename 1 ten as 10 ones.	Subtract the ones.	Subtract the tens.
51 −23	⁴¹¹ 5̷1̷ −23	⁴¹¹ 5̷1̷ −23 8	⁴¹¹ 5̷1̷ −23 difference →28

Subtract.

98 − 89 9	20 − 3	11 − 2	46 − 29	64 − 38
71 − 35	60 − 15	22 − 13	56 − 28	44 − 17
10 − 6	53 − 25	74 − 26	51 − 4	75 − 39
42 − 27	75 − 46	82 − 36	51 − 25	97 − 49
50 − 14	82 − 45	55 − 47	72 − 48	90 − 41
76 − 58	31 − 7	43 − 34	62 − 27	92 − 36

Lesson 3.3 Problem Solving

Solve each problem.

Marti catches 23 in the first pond.

She catches 14 in the second pond.

How many more does

she catch in the first pond? _____9_____

There are 42 in the tree.

There are 33 at the feeder.

How many more are in the tree? _____

Craig finds 13 .

Zach finds 30 .

How many more does Zach find? _____

There were 28 in the park. Some left.

There were 19 remaining in the park. $28 -$ _____ $= 19$

How many left the park? _____

There are 32 in the barn.

There are 27 in the yard.

How many more are in the barn? _____

Lesson 3.3 Problem Solving

Solve each problem.

Freddie finds 33 .

Tina finds 28 .

How many more does Freddie find? __5__

$$\begin{array}{r} \overset{2}{\cancel{3}}\,\overset{13}{\cancel{3}} \\ -\ 2\ 8 \\ \hline 5 \end{array}$$

Adam picks up 25  on Monday and 27  on Tuesday.

19 of the are broken.

How many of the are not broken? _____

Becky has 31 .

She eats 8 .

How many does she have left? _____

William has 26 .

He gives some to a friend.

Now, he has only 18 .

How many did William give to his friend? _____

$$26 - \underline{\hspace{1.5cm}} = 18$$

Connie counts 42 .

Annie counts 27 .

How many more does Connie count? _____

Check What You Learned

Subtracting 2-Digit Numbers (With Renaming)

Subtract.

83	68	73	30	65
− 44	− 59	− 38	− 24	− 39

53	15	47	75	26
− 35	− 9	− 18	− 37	− 18

84	60	76	52	42
− 46	− 34	− 29	− 43	− 27

Solve each problem.

Ayisha buys 60 .

51 of them are ripe.

How many of the are not ripe? _____

Nick picks 42 .

He sells 18 at the farm stand.

How many does Nick have left? _____

42 − 18 = _____

The farm stand sells 37 on Saturday

and 29 on Sunday. How many more

 does it sell on Saturday? _____

Mid-Test Chapters 1–3

Subtract.

5 − 3	11 − 4	15 − 5	13 − 5	17 − 3	8 − 1
3 − 1	13 − 6	19 − 6	6 − 4	16 − 3	13 − 1
4 − 1	5 − 4	7 − 6	17 − 4	14 − 1	9 − 6
17 − 2	3 − 2	18 − 2	17 − 8	10 − 1	6 − 2
12 − 9	11 − 5	17 − 1	18 − 6	20 − 4	6 − 5
11 − 1	15 − 4	9 − 4	8 − 2	9 − 2	5 − 2

Mid-Test Chapters 1–3

Solve each problem.

There are 20 🧢.

There are 8 👒.

How many more 🧢 ? _____

There are 12 🥄 on the table.

There are 6 🥄 in the drawer.

How many more 🥄 are on the table? _____

There are 18 🍎.

We eat 9 🍎.

How many 🍎 are left? _____

There are 16 🦁 under a tree.

9 🦁 walk away.

How many 🦁 are left? _____

Tanya has 11 🌼.

Curtis has 7 🌼.

How many more 🌼 does Tanya have? _____

Mid-Test Chapters 1–3

Subtract.

97 − 91	98 − 13	60 − 31	65 − 50	74 − 37	76 − 46
46 − 35	64 − 56	72 − 34	86 − 54	97 − 66	36 − 32
65 − 24	99 − 11	55 − 38	70 − 42	78 − 55	84 − 37
94 − 38	65 − 16	71 − 35	37 − 17	88 − 20	85 − 59
53 − 45	75 − 61	95 − 39	92 − 46	66 − 9	35 − 21
88 − 60	50 − 14	52 − 28	69 − 42	90 − 45	66 − 56

CHAPTERS 1–3 MID-TEST

Mid-Test Chapters 1–3

SHOW YOUR WORK

Solve each problem.

Emil has 63 .

He lends 11 to Jeff.

How many does Emil have left? _____

Terrence has 24 .

Bella has 91 .

How many more does Bella have? _____

An apple costs 90¢.

An orange costs 75¢.

How much more does an apple cost? _____¢

The earth club plants 86 on Saturday

and 53 on Sunday.

How many more did they plant on Saturday? _____

The earth club plants 45 .

24 of the  are red. 13 of the are yellow.

How many are not red or yellow? _____

CHAPTERS 1–3 MID-TEST

NAME _____

Check What You Know

Subtracting from 3-Digit Numbers

Write the number shown by the blocks. Then, use the blocks to help you solve the subtraction problems.

 = _____

382 − 100 = _____   382 − 282 = _____

382 − 200 = _____   382 − 182 = _____

382 − 300 = _____   382 − 82 = _____

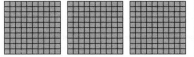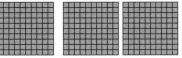 = _____

749 − 200 = _____   749 − 549 = _____

749 − 400 = _____   749 − 349 = _____

749 − 600 = _____   749 − 49 = _____

Count backward by ones.   463, _____, _____, 460, _____

Count backward by fives.   880, 875, _____, _____, _____

Count backward by tens.   295, _____, 275, _____, _____

Count backward by hundreds. 763, 663, _____, _____, _____

Write the number that is 100 less.

587 _____   299 _____   152 _____

Write the number that is 10 less.

426 _____   988 _____   675 _____

Check What You Know

Subtracting from 3-Digit Numbers

Subtract.

123	87	545	79	187	782
− 15	− 23	− 35	− 63	− 93	− 143

898	763	981	725	805	120
− 454	− 321	− 133	− 125	− 73	− 80

76	87	72	153	763	876
− 41	− 35	− 35	− 92	− 154	− 450

138	192	712	392	510	692
− 52	− 175	− 92	− 286	− 347	− 486

120	198	175	908	798	586
− 45	− 79	− 84	− 67	− 104	− 62

573	278	779	741	944	525
− 110	− 178	− 66	− 514	− 345	− 430

Lesson 4.1 Using Place Value 150 through 199

Use the hundreds, tens, and ones blocks to help you solve the subtraction problems.

 = 153

$$153 - 100 = 53 \qquad 153 - 3 = 150$$
$$153 - 50 = 103 \qquad 153 - 53 = 100$$

$165 - 100 = \underline{65}$

$165 - 60 = \underline{105}$

$165 - 5 = \underline{160}$

$165 - 65 = \underline{100}$

$178 - 100 = \underline{\qquad}$

$178 - 70 = \underline{\qquad}$

$178 - 8 = \underline{\qquad}$

$178 - 78 = \underline{\qquad}$

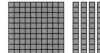

$184 - 100 = \underline{\qquad}$

$184 - 80 = \underline{\qquad}$

$184 - 4 = \underline{\qquad}$

$184 - 84 = \underline{\qquad}$

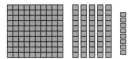

$158 - 100 = \underline{\qquad}$

$158 - 50 = \underline{\qquad}$

$158 - 8 = \underline{\qquad}$

$158 - 58 = \underline{\qquad}$

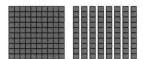

$170 - 100 = \underline{\qquad}$

$170 - 70 = \underline{\qquad}$

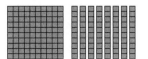

$180 - 100 = \underline{\qquad}$

$180 - 80 = \underline{\qquad}$

Lesson 4.2 Using Place Value 200 through 399

Use the hundreds, tens, and ones blocks to help you solve the subtraction problems.

 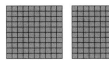 = 336

336 − 100 = 236   336 − 236 = 100
336 − 200 = 136   336 − 136 = 200
336 − 300 = 36   336 − 36 = 300

234 − 100 = _134_

234 − 200 = _34_

234 − 134 = _100_

234 − 34 = _200_

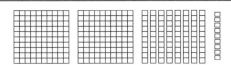

289 − 100 = _____

289 − 200 = _____

289 − 189 = _____

289 − 89 = _____

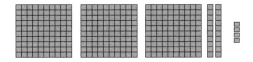

324 − 100 = _____

324 − 200 = _____

324 − 300 = _____

324 − 224 = _____

324 − 124 = _____

324 − 24 = _____

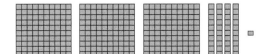

341 − 100 = _____

341 − 200 = _____

341 − 300 = _____

341 − 241 = _____

341 − 141 = _____

341 − 41 = _____

Lesson 4.3 Using Place Value 400 through 699

Use the hundreds, tens, and ones blocks to help you solve the subtraction problems.

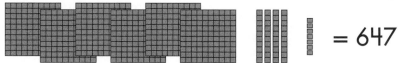 = 647

647 − 100 = 547   647 − 447 = 200
647 − 300 = 347   647 − 247 = 400
647 − 500 = 147   647 − 47 = 600

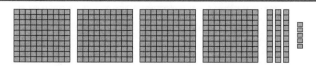

435 − 100 = _335_

435 − 200 = _235_

435 − 400 = _35_

435 − 335 = _100_

435 − 235 = _200_

435 − 35 = _400_

514 − 100 = _____

514 − 300 = _____

514 − 500 = _____

514 − 414 = _____

514 − 214 = _____

514 − 14 = _____

671 − 200 = _____

671 − 400 = _____

671 − 600 = _____

671 − 571 = _____

671 − 371 = _____

671 − 71 = _____

433 − 100 = _____

433 − 200 = _____

433 − 400 = _____

433 − 333 = _____

433 − 133 = _____

433 − 33 = _____

Lesson 4.4 Using Place Value 700 through 999

Use the hundreds, tens, and ones blocks to help you solve the subtraction problems.

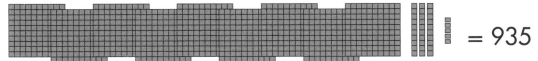 = 935

$935 - 300 = 635$ $935 - 435 = 500$
$935 - 500 = 435$ $935 - 235 = 700$
$935 - 700 = 235$ $935 - 35 = 900$

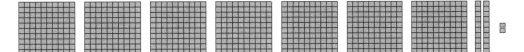

$722 - 200 =$ _____ $722 - 322 =$ _____

$722 - 400 =$ _____ $722 - 122 =$ _____

$722 - 600 =$ _____ $722 - 22 =$ _____

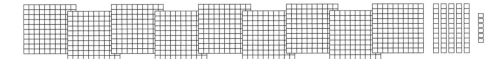

$956 - 300 =$ _____ $956 - 456 =$ _____

$956 - 600 =$ _____ $956 - 256 =$ _____

$956 - 900 =$ _____ $956 - 56 =$ _____

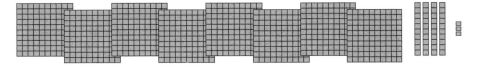

$843 - 300 =$ _____ $843 - 343 =$ _____

$843 - 500 =$ _____ $843 - 243 =$ _____

$843 - 700 =$ _____ $843 - 43 =$ _____

Lesson 4.5 Skip Counting Back

Count backward by ones.

317, 316, 315, _____, 313, _____, _____, 310

422, 421, _____, 419, _____, _____, 416, 415

Count backward by fives.

635, 630, _____, _____, 615, 610, _____ 600

820, _____, _____, _____, 800, 795, 790, 785

475, 470, _____, _____, 455, _____, _____, 440

Count backward by tens.

650, 640, _____ _____, 610, _____, 590, 580

700, 690, _____, 670, _____, 650, 640, _____

320, _____, 300, _____, _____, 270, 260, _____

Count backward by hundreds.

_____, 600, 500, _____, _____, 200, 100, 0

900, 800, 700, 600, _____, 400, _____, _____

800, _____, 600, _____, _____, _____, 200, 100

Lesson 4.5 Skip Counting Back

Count backward by hundreds. Start at 950.

950, _____, 750, _____, _____, 450, _____

Count backward by ones. Start at 773.

773, 772, 771, _____, _____, _____, _____

Count backward by tens. Start at 435.

435, 425, _____, _____, 395, _____, _____

Count backward by hundreds. Start at 827.

827, 727, _____, _____, 427, _____, _____

Count backward by fives. Start at 185.

185, _____, _____, _____, _____, 160, 155

Count backward by ones. Start at 999.

999, 998, 997, _____, _____, _____, _____

Count backward by fives. Start at 300.

300, 295, _____ _____, 280, _____, _____

Count backward by tens. Start at 610.

610, _____, 590, _____, _____, 560, _____

Lesson 4.6 Mentally Subtract 100

When you subtract 100 from a three-digit number, only the number in the hundreds place changes. It is one less. The numbers in the tens and ones places stay the same.

$$654 - 100 = 554$$

$$6 - 1 = 5$$

Subtract 100 from each number. Solve the problem only in your mind. Write the number in the thought bubble.

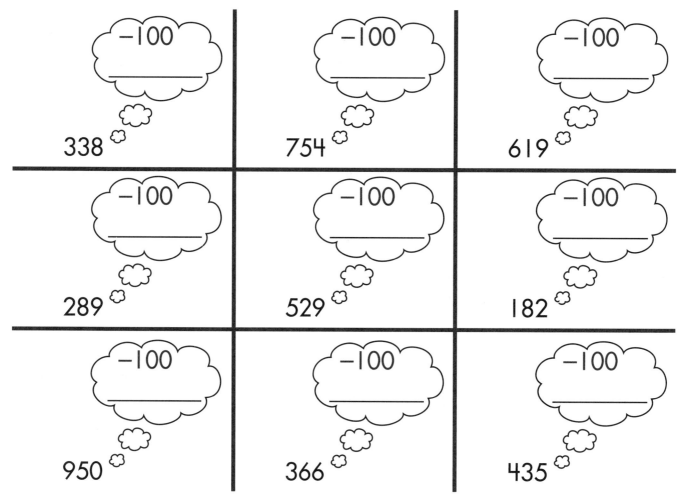

338

754

619

289

529

182

950

366

435

Lesson 4.7 Mentally Subtract 10

When you subtract 10 from a three-digit number, only the number in the tens place changes. It is one less. The numbers in the hundreds and ones places stay the same.

382 − 10 = 372
8 − 1 = 7

Subtract 10 from each number. Solve the problem only in your mind. Write the number in the thought bubble.

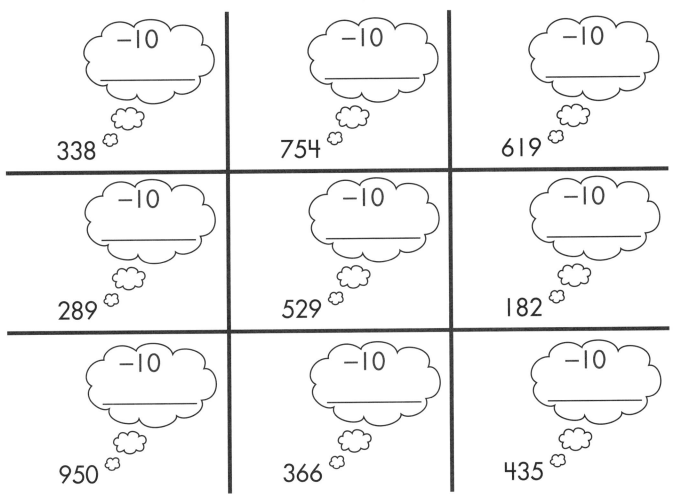

−10	−10	−10
338	754	619
−10	−10	−10
289	529	182
−10	−10	−10
950	366	435

Lesson 4.8 Subtracting 2 Digits from 3 Digits

	Subtract the ones. ↓	To subtract the tens, rename the 1 hundred and 2 tens as 12 tens.	Subtract the tens. ↓	
$\begin{array}{r} 125 \\ -\ 84 \\ \hline \end{array}$	$\begin{array}{r} 125 \\ -\ 84 \\ \hline 1 \end{array}$	$\begin{array}{r} \overset{12}{\cancel{1}\cancel{2}}5 \\ -\ 84 \\ \hline 1 \end{array}$	$\begin{array}{r} \overset{12}{\cancel{1}\cancel{2}}5 \\ -\ 84 \\ \hline 41 \end{array}$	minuend subtrahend difference

Subtract.

$\begin{array}{r} 113 \\ -\ 33 \\ \hline 80 \end{array}$
$\begin{array}{r} 121 \\ -\ 60 \\ \hline \end{array}$
$\begin{array}{r} 195 \\ -\ 44 \\ \hline \end{array}$
$\begin{array}{r} 122 \\ -\ 11 \\ \hline \end{array}$
$\begin{array}{r} 147 \\ -\ 53 \\ \hline \end{array}$

$\begin{array}{r} 143 \\ -\ 62 \\ \hline \end{array}$
$\begin{array}{r} 180 \\ -\ 70 \\ \hline \end{array}$
$\begin{array}{r} 119 \\ -\ 15 \\ \hline \end{array}$
$\begin{array}{r} 123 \\ -\ 12 \\ \hline \end{array}$
$\begin{array}{r} 186 \\ -\ 65 \\ \hline \end{array}$

$\begin{array}{r} 154 \\ -\ 13 \\ \hline \end{array}$
$\begin{array}{r} 127 \\ -\ 83 \\ \hline \end{array}$
$\begin{array}{r} 187 \\ -\ 67 \\ \hline \end{array}$
$\begin{array}{r} 135 \\ -\ 42 \\ \hline \end{array}$
$\begin{array}{r} 115 \\ -\ 24 \\ \hline \end{array}$

$\begin{array}{r} 132 \\ -\ 51 \\ \hline \end{array}$
$\begin{array}{r} 177 \\ -\ 43 \\ \hline \end{array}$
$\begin{array}{r} 192 \\ -\ 71 \\ \hline \end{array}$
$\begin{array}{r} 186 \\ -\ 92 \\ \hline \end{array}$
$\begin{array}{r} 134 \\ -\ 72 \\ \hline \end{array}$

$\begin{array}{r} 129 \\ -\ 86 \\ \hline \end{array}$
$\begin{array}{r} 176 \\ -\ 75 \\ \hline \end{array}$
$\begin{array}{r} 120 \\ -\ 40 \\ \hline \end{array}$
$\begin{array}{r} 194 \\ -\ 53 \\ \hline \end{array}$
$\begin{array}{r} 189 \\ -\ 62 \\ \hline \end{array}$

Lesson 4.8 Subtracting 2 Digits from 3 Digits

Rename 5 tens and 3 ones as 4 tens and 13 ones.	Subtract the ones. ↓	Rename 1 hundred and 4 tens as 14 tens.	Subtract the tens. ↓	

153
− 65
	⁴¹³
	1 5̶3̶
	− 65
		⁴¹³
		1 5̶3̶
		− 65
		    8
			¹⁴¹³
			1 5̶3̶
			− 65
			    8
				¹⁴¹³
				1 5̶3̶ minuend
				− 65 subtrahend
				  8 8 difference

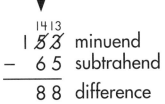

Subtract.

162 − 73 89	175 − 97	182 − 94	103 − 17	116 − 39
174 − 95	147 − 68	132 − 65	115 − 49	107 − 39
101 − 75	100 − 92	127 − 79	133 − 44	142 − 73
141 − 63	137 − 79	142 − 73	153 − 67	155 − 96
100 − 72	106 − 48	117 − 88	124 − 66	163 − 89

Lesson 4.9 Subtraction Practice

Subtract.

132 − 71	196 − 87	165 − 59	163 − 71	119 − 29
106 − 51	100 − 29	153 − 69	147 − 88	192 − 75
175 − 95	169 − 99	142 − 37	140 − 93	131 − 57
167 − 76	173 − 82	192 − 95	143 − 77	126 − 54
117 − 26	100 − 33	175 − 46	142 − 57	136 − 47
176 − 89	143 − 54	140 − 39	173 − 75	163 − 92

Lesson 4.9 Subtraction Practice

Subtract.

144 − 86	122 − 31	191 − 75	175 − 93	144 − 65
121 − 37	106 − 42	165 − 43	162 − 47	181 − 57
106 − 99	127 − 49	136 − 58	124 − 75	143 − 52
685 − 96	444 − 67	612 − 22	786 − 19	950 − 99
865 − 92	710 − 7	475 − 89	627 − 10	751 − 93
509 − 75	696 − 5	815 − 25	545 − 57	115 − 72

Lesson 4.10 Subtracting 3-Digit Numbers

Rename 2 tens and 1 one as 1 ten and 11 ones. Then, subtract the ones.	Rename 6 hundreds and 1 ten as 5 hundreds and 11 tens. Then, subtract the tens.	Subtract the hundreds.

$$\begin{array}{r} 6\,2\,1 \\ -2\,5\,9 \\ \hline \end{array}$$

$$\begin{array}{r} 6\,2\,1 \\ -2\,5\,9 \\ \hline 2 \end{array}$$

$$\begin{array}{r} 6\,2\,1 \\ -2\,5\,9 \\ \hline 6\,2 \end{array}$$

$$\begin{array}{r} 6\,2\,1 \\ -2\,5\,9 \\ \hline 3\,6\,2 \end{array}$$ minuend subtrahend difference

Subtract.

321 −109 *212*	745 −152	639 −150	830 −710	626 −146
729 −321	657 −451	386 −107	411 −305	486 −109
983 −652	971 −572	876 −357	549 −360	721 −144
256 −142	347 −139	725 −196	863 −692	980 −532

Lesson 4.10 Subtracting 3-Digit Numbers

Rename 1 ten and 3 ones as 0 tens and 13 ones. Then, subtract the ones.	Rename 5 hundreds and 0 tens as 4 hundreds and 10 tens. Then, subtract the tens.	Subtract the hundreds.

$$\begin{array}{r} 513 \\ -125 \\ \hline \end{array}$$
$$\begin{array}{r} \overset{0\ 13}{5\cancel{1}\cancel{3}} \\ -125 \\ \hline 8 \end{array}$$
$$\begin{array}{r} \overset{10}{\underset{4\ \cancel{0}\ 13}{5\cancel{1}\cancel{3}}} \\ -125 \\ \hline 88 \end{array}$$
$$\begin{array}{r} \overset{10}{\underset{4\ \cancel{0}\ 13}{5\cancel{1}\cancel{3}}} \\ -125 \\ \hline 388 \end{array}$$ minuend subtrahend difference

Subtract.

$$\begin{array}{r} 543 \\ -457 \\ \hline \end{array} \qquad \begin{array}{r} 762 \\ -135 \\ \hline \end{array} \qquad \begin{array}{r} 132 \\ -107 \\ \hline \end{array} \qquad \begin{array}{r} 921 \\ -571 \\ \hline \end{array} \qquad \begin{array}{r} 631 \\ -545 \\ \hline \end{array}$$

$$\begin{array}{r} 531 \\ -250 \\ \hline \end{array} \qquad \begin{array}{r} 720 \\ -371 \\ \hline \end{array} \qquad \begin{array}{r} 582 \\ -357 \\ \hline \end{array} \qquad \begin{array}{r} 793 \\ -457 \\ \hline \end{array} \qquad \begin{array}{r} 612 \\ -483 \\ \hline \end{array}$$

$$\begin{array}{r} 543 \\ -206 \\ \hline \end{array} \qquad \begin{array}{r} 432 \\ -257 \\ \hline \end{array} \qquad \begin{array}{r} 710 \\ -512 \\ \hline \end{array} \qquad \begin{array}{r} 432 \\ -119 \\ \hline \end{array} \qquad \begin{array}{r} 186 \\ -107 \\ \hline \end{array}$$

$$\begin{array}{r} 712 \\ -347 \\ \hline \end{array} \qquad \begin{array}{r} 690 \\ -320 \\ \hline \end{array} \qquad \begin{array}{r} 451 \\ -253 \\ \hline \end{array} \qquad \begin{array}{r} 512 \\ -308 \\ \hline \end{array} \qquad \begin{array}{r} 861 \\ -172 \\ \hline \end{array}$$

Lesson 4.11 Subtraction Practice

Subtract.

142	192	543	192	190
−131	−127	−121	−154	−150

182	396	540	513	312
−159	−185	−375	−211	−192

412	790	674	700	690
−306	−205	−556	−310	−541

898	412	775	962	829
−844	−340	−436	−841	−394

796	710	971	583	710
−318	−696	−320	−421	−190

Lesson 4.11 Subtraction Practice

Subtract.

711 −547	786 −457	210 −102	232 −144	457 −310
740 −310	862 −456	610 −232	695 −159	869 −341
934 −281	752 −557	745 −494	658 −237	674 −164
868 −256	430 −253	580 −371	853 −359	797 −191
711 −278	721 −135	864 −724	935 −691	722 −429

Check What You Learned

Subtracting from 3-Digit Numbers

Write the number shown by the blocks. Then, use the blocks to help you solve the subtraction problems.

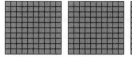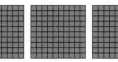 = _____

568 − 200 = _____   568 − 368 = _____

568 − 400 = _____   568 − 168 = _____

568 − 500 = _____   568 − 68 = _____

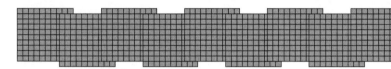 = _____

906 − 300 = _____   906 − 706 = _____

906 − 600 = _____   906 − 506 = _____

906 − 900 = _____   906 − 6 = _____

Count backward by ones.   111, _____, _____, 108, _____

Count backward by fives.   660, 655, _____, _____, _____

Count backward by tens.   394, _____, 374, _____, _____

Count backward by hundreds. 855, 755, _____, _____, _____

Write the number that is 100 less.

850 _____   172 _____   549 _____

Write the number that is 10 less.

822 _____   395 _____   412 _____

Check What You Learned

Subtracting from 3-Digit Numbers

Subtract.

172	192	174	120	310	293
− 35	− 86	− 96	− 80	− 40	−107

986	862	352	187	647	547
−698	−245	−121	− 72	−253	−183

662	708	456	882	753	712
−503	−231	−269	−199	−268	−543

185	216	156	687	923	824
−153	− 53	− 40	−246	−814	−487

905	688	648	906	648	916
− 26	−141	−141	− 27	−597	−411

793	643	997	852	158	250
−144	−508	−398	−399	− 63	−136

NAME _____

 Check What You Know

Using Subtraction

Subtract. Check each answer by writing an addition problem. The first one is done for you.

```
  1 2 6        8 6        5 4 2        9 6 0         9 7
-   7 4      -  1 7      - 1 5 0      -   2 6      -  8 2
─────────    ────────    ────────     ────────     ────────
    5 2
+   7 4
─────────
  1 2 6
```

```
  5 1 2        2 0        4 8 8         4 9        6 1 4
-   1 8      -  1 6      - 1 9 9      -   2 5      - 2 7 6
─────────    ────────    ────────     ────────     ────────
```

Write the missing number in each equation.

```
    9 9        4 8 7        1 5 6       ┌──────┐
-  ┌────┐    - 2 5 6      - ┌────┐      │      │
   │    │     ────────      │    │      └──────┘
   └────┘     ┌──────┐      └──────┘    -   5 8
─────────     │      │     ─────────    ─────────
    4 5       └──────┘      1 3 1        7 1 5
```

```
  6 3 5      ┌──────┐        8 1 6        4 2 2
-  ┌────┐    │      │      - 6 2 0      - ┌────┐
   │    │    └──────┘       ─────────     │    │
   └────┘    -   5 2        ┌──────┐      └──────┘
─────────    ─────────      │      │     ─────────
  1 0 0        4 0 0        └──────┘       4 2 2
```

Check What You Know

Using Subtraction

Measure each object. Tell how much longer one object is than the other.

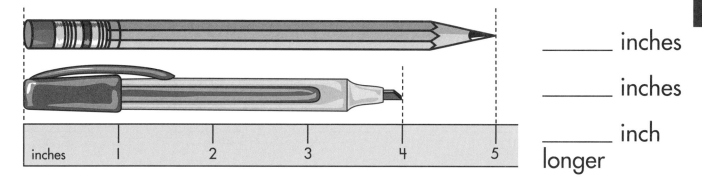

_____ inches

_____ inches

_____ inch
longer

Write the money amounts. Subtract.

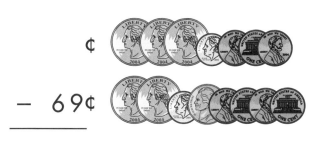

58¢

− ___¢

_____

___¢

− 69¢

Solve the problems.

Marco's bean plant grew to 16 inches tall.

Julisa's bean plant grew to 21 inches tall.

How much taller is Julisa's plant? _____ inches

Sydney found 2 quarters, 1 nickel, and 3 pennies.

She bought a cup of lemonade for 45¢

How much money did she have left? _____¢

Lesson 5.1 Checking Subtraction with Addition

To check

982 − 657 = 325,

add 657 to 325.

$$\begin{array}{r} 982 \\ -657 \\ \hline 325 \\ +657 \\ \hline 982 \end{array}$$

These should be the same.

Subtract. Check each answer.

$$\begin{array}{r} 720 \\ -150 \\ \hline 570 \\ +150 \\ \hline 720 \end{array}$$

$$\begin{array}{r} 321 \\ -83 \\ \hline \end{array}$$

$$\begin{array}{r} 125 \\ -92 \\ \hline \end{array}$$

$$\begin{array}{r} 983 \\ -657 \\ \hline \end{array}$$

$$\begin{array}{r} 456 \\ -291 \\ \hline \end{array}$$

$$\begin{array}{r} 300 \\ -179 \\ \hline \end{array}$$

$$\begin{array}{r} 119 \\ -104 \\ \hline \end{array}$$

$$\begin{array}{r} 423 \\ -197 \\ \hline \end{array}$$

$$\begin{array}{r} 259 \\ -147 \\ \hline \end{array}$$

$$\begin{array}{r} 592 \\ -463 \\ \hline \end{array}$$

$$\begin{array}{r} 519 \\ -120 \\ \hline \end{array}$$

$$\begin{array}{r} 540 \\ -320 \\ \hline \end{array}$$

$$\begin{array}{r} 192 \\ -86 \\ \hline \end{array}$$

$$\begin{array}{r} 710 \\ -447 \\ \hline \end{array}$$

$$\begin{array}{r} 683 \\ -419 \\ \hline \end{array}$$

$$\begin{array}{r} 719 \\ -532 \\ \hline \end{array}$$

$$\begin{array}{r} 919 \\ -457 \\ \hline \end{array}$$

$$\begin{array}{r} 687 \\ -250 \\ \hline \end{array}$$

$$\begin{array}{r} 912 \\ -609 \\ \hline \end{array}$$

$$\begin{array}{r} 542 \\ -327 \\ \hline \end{array}$$

Lesson 5.2 Checking Addition with Subtraction

To check

215 + 109 = 324,

subtract 109 from 324.

```
  2 1 5
+ 1 0 9
-------
  3 2 4      These should be the same.
- 1 0 9
-------
  2 1 5
```

Add. Check each answer.

```
   1 5 7        7 1 9        3 1 2        2 1 3        3 0 6
 + 2 1 2      + 1 8 2      + 1 0 5      + 5 1 9      + 2 1 5
 -------      -------      -------      -------      -------
   3 6 9
 - 2 1 2
 -------
   1 5 7
```

```
   7 1 0        3 5 7        7 1 2        6 1 4        3 1 2
 + 2 1 8      + 2 4 9      + 2 6 3      + 2 9 1      +   8 5
 -------      -------      -------      -------      -------
```

```
   3 0 0        5 9 1        6 1 2        4 2 5        4 1 1
 + 5 4 7      + 1 2 0      + 3 1 9      + 1 2 5      + 1 2 0
 -------      -------      -------      -------      -------
```

```
   8 6 3        4 5 9        6 0 3        7 1 1        2 5 2
 +   9 2      + 1 3 0      + 2 0 9      + 1 9 1      + 1 3 0
 -------      -------      -------      -------      -------
```

Lesson 5.3 Finding an Unknown Number

Use subtraction and addition to find the missing number in each equation. Write the missing number in the box.

$$\begin{array}{r} \boxed{} \\ -\ 7 \\ \hline 13 \end{array} \qquad \begin{array}{r} 100 \\ -\ \boxed{} \\ \hline 63 \end{array} \qquad \begin{array}{r} 163 \\ -\ \boxed{} \\ \hline 129 \end{array} \qquad \begin{array}{r} \boxed{} \\ -\ 52 \\ \hline 723 \end{array}$$

$$\begin{array}{r} 144 \\ -\ \boxed{} \\ \hline 144 \end{array} \qquad \begin{array}{r} 996 \\ -380 \\ \hline \boxed{} \end{array} \qquad \begin{array}{r} \boxed{} \\ -\ 58 \\ \hline 100 \end{array} \qquad \begin{array}{r} 79 \\ -\ \boxed{} \\ \hline 77 \end{array}$$

$$\begin{array}{r} 226 \\ -195 \\ \hline \boxed{} \end{array} \qquad \begin{array}{r} \boxed{} \\ -\ 99 \\ \hline 900 \end{array} \qquad \begin{array}{r} 783 \\ -\ \boxed{} \\ \hline 550 \end{array} \qquad \begin{array}{r} \boxed{} \\ -\ 84 \\ \hline 132 \end{array}$$

$$\begin{array}{r} 65 \\ -\ 9 \\ \hline \boxed{} \end{array} \qquad \begin{array}{r} \boxed{} \\ -\ 10 \\ \hline 90 \end{array} \qquad \begin{array}{r} 55 \\ -\ \boxed{} \\ \hline 49 \end{array} \qquad \begin{array}{r} \boxed{} \\ -133 \\ \hline 281 \end{array}$$

Lesson 5.3 Finding an Unknown Number

In each equation, a symbol stands for a missing number. Write the missing number beside the symbol at the bottom of the page.

88 − ✳ = 76

622 − ✝ = 254

458 − ❤ = 451

✳ − 12 = 0

86 − 86 = ◉

☺ − 33 = 966

200 − ⚡ = 171

778 − ◉ = 778

100 − 93 = ❤

100 − ⚡ = 71

★ − 13 = 37

▲ − 95 = 104

220 − ▲ = 21

800 − ★ = 750

☺ − 700 = 299

✝ − 81 = 287

Lesson 5.4 How Much Longer?

Measure each object. Tell how much longer one object is than the other.

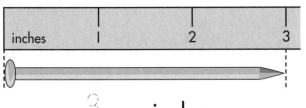 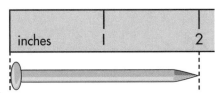

_____3_____ inches   _____2_____ inches   __1__ inch longer

$$\begin{array}{r} 3 \\ -2 \\ \hline 1 \end{array}$$

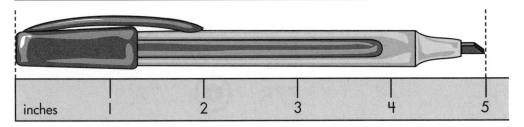

_____ inches

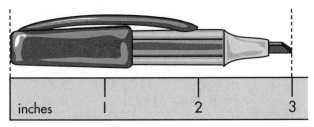

_____ inches

_____ inches longer

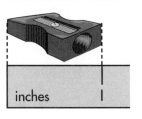 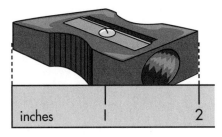

_____ inch

_____ inches

_____ inch longer

Lesson 5.4 How Much Longer?

Measure each object. Tell how much longer one object is than the other.

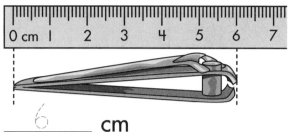 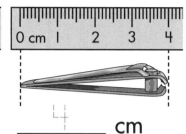

$$\begin{array}{r} 6 \\ -\ 4 \\ \hline 2 \end{array}$$

__6__ cm   __4__ cm   __2__ cm longer

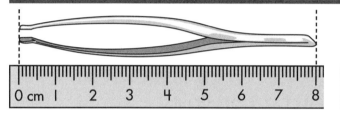 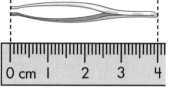

_____ cm   _____ cm   ___ cm longer

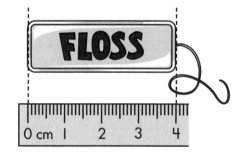 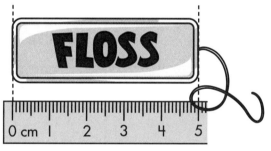

_____ cm   _____ cm   ___ cm longer

_____ cm   _____ cm   ___ cm longer

Lesson 5.5 Subtracting Money

A banana costs	An apple costs	An orange costs	A melon costs

35¢	20¢	33¢	85¢

Which fruit costs the most? _____

Which fruit costs the least? _____

A melon costs $\quad$ 85¢ An orange costs $\quad$ −33¢ A melon costs this much more. $\quad$ 52¢	An orange costs $\qquad$ ¢ An apple costs $\quad$ − $\qquad$ ¢ An orange costs this much more. $\qquad$ ¢
A banana costs $\qquad$ ¢ An apple costs $\quad$ − $\qquad$ ¢ A banana costs this much more. $\qquad$ ¢	A melon costs $\qquad$ ¢ An apple costs $\quad$ − $\qquad$ ¢ A melon costs this much more. $\qquad$ ¢
A melon costs $\qquad$ ¢ A banana costs $\quad$ − $\qquad$ ¢ A melon costs this much more. $\qquad$ ¢	A banana costs $\qquad$ ¢ An orange costs $\quad$ − $\qquad$ ¢ A banana costs this much more. $\qquad$ ¢

Lesson 5.5 Subtracting Money

One dollar is equal to 100 cents.

A pencil costs	A pen costs	A marker costs	A crayon costs

30¢	32¢	42¢	24¢

Paid with one dollar   100¢
Bought one pencil   − 30¢
The change is   70¢

Paid with one dollar   100¢
Bought one crayon   − ____¢
The change is   ¢

Paid with one dollar   100¢
Bought one marker   − ____¢
The change is   ¢

Paid with one dollar   100¢
Bought one pen   − ____¢
The change is   ¢

Paid with one dollar   100¢
Bought two pens   − ____¢
The change is   ¢

Paid with one dollar   100¢
Bought three crayons − ____¢
The change is   ¢

Lesson 5.6 Problem Solving

Solve each problem.

Hannah's dog can jump 15 inches into the air.

Maricela's dog can jump 26 inches into the air.

How much higher can Maricela's dog jump? _____ inches

Jordan grew 18 centimeters this year.

Kyleigh grew 6 centimeters this year.

How much more did Jordan grow? _____ cm

The blue jump rope is 62 inches long.

The pink jump rope is 78 inches long.

How much longer is the pink rope? _____ inches

Matthew's dad is 70 inches tall.

Orlando's dad is 80 inches tall.

How much taller is the taller dad? _____ inches

In the morning, an ant traveled 187 centimeters.

In the afternoon, the ant traveled 312 centimeters.

How much farther did the ant travel in the afternoon?

_____ cm

Lesson 5.6 Problem Solving

Solve each problem.

At a food stand, a bean burrito costs 99¢

A soft chicken taco costs 79¢

How much more is the burrito? _____ ¢

Caleb had three quarters in his pocket.

He bought a postcard for 36¢

How much money does he have left? _____ ¢

Bonnie has two dimes and six pennies.

At the carnival, she wants to buy a ticket for 25¢

Does Bonnie have enough money? _____

Dad gave Roland one dollar.

Roland will spend half of the money and save the other half.

How much will Roland save? _____ ¢

Cassie's mother gave her money to spend at the book fair: 1 dollar bill, 2 quarters, 4 dimes, 1 nickel, and 5 pennies.

Cassie wants to buy a book that costs 3 dollars.

Does Cassie have enough money? _____

Check What You Learned

Using Subtraction

Subtract. Check each answer by writing an addition problem. The first one is done for you.

```
    86          508         52          171         300
  -  9         - 99        -  6        - 55        - 42
  _____     _____    _____    _____    _____
    77
  +  9
  --------
    86
```

```
    53          256         629          87          711
  - 17         -188        -  29        -  4        -276
  _____     _____    _____     _____    _____
```

Write the missing number in each equation.

```
    802         480          99          [    ]
  -[    ]     -315         -[  ]        -  72
  _____    _____     _____     _____
    125       [    ]          8          228
```

```
    456         [    ]        100          809
  -[    ]     -  52         -  58        -[    ]
  _____    _____     _____     _____
     81          638        [    ]         700
```

Check What You Learned

Using Subtraction

Measure each object. Tell how much longer one object is than the other.

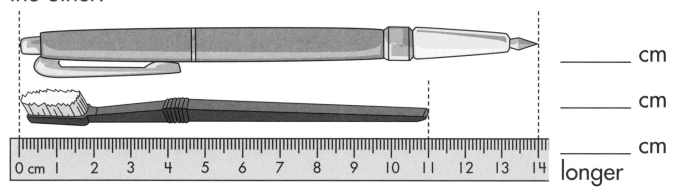

_____ cm

_____ cm

_____ cm
longer

Write the money amounts. Subtract.

$$100¢$$
$$- \quad ¢$$
_____

$$\quad ¢$$
$$- \ 21¢$$
_____

Solve the problems.

The bulletin board is 122 centimeters long.

The paper is 150 centimeters long.

How much paper should be cut off to fit the board?

_____ cm

Thomas has 5 dimes, 1 nickel, and 8 pennies.

He wants to buy a postcard for 55¢

Does he have enough money? _____

Final Test Chapters 1–5

Subtract.

79 − 43	7 − 2	18 − 9	43 − 15	12 − 3	68 − 15
30 − 19	15 − 8	10 − 3	46 − 36	3 − 0	43 − 6
14 − 6	8 − 8	56 − 44	72 − 35	17 − 9	9 − 4
79 − 36	15 − 9	75 − 36	7 − 7	68 − 22	17 − 8
11 − 3	82 − 79	4 − 3	50 − 23	9 − 5	78 − 55
52 − 21	19 − 5	99 − 20	20 − 7	61 − 40	80 − 9

Final Test Chapters 1–5

Solve each problem.

Jenny is reading a book that is 98 pages long.
She has read 47 pages so far.
How many pages does Jenny have left to read? _____

47 + _____ = 98

Addison bakes 14 loaves of bread.
After she gives some away, she has 6 left.
How many loaves of bread did Addison give away? _____

14 – _____ = 6

Courtney had some fabric.
Becca gave her 12 more feet of fabric.
Now, Courtney has 65 feet of fabric.
How many feet of fabric did Courtney have to start with? _____

_____ + 12 = 65

There are 12 campers in the lake for an afternoon swim.
6 more campers join them.
If 9 of the campers get out of the lake,
how many campers are left swimming in the lake? _____

Kayla raked leaves in her front yard for 55 minutes.
She raked leaves in her backyard for 26 minutes.
How much longer did Kayla spend raking in her front yard?
_____ minutes

Final Test Chapters 1–5

Write the number shown by the blocks. Then, use the blocks to help you solve the subtraction problems.

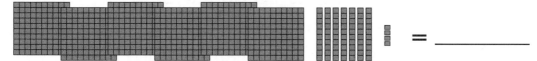 = _____

674 – 200 = _____   674 – 374 = _____

674 – 400 = _____   674 – 174 = _____

674 – 600 = _____   674 – 74 = _____

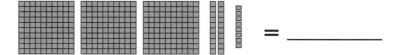 = _____

328 – 100 = _____   328 – 228 = _____

328 – 200 = _____   328 – 128 = _____

328 – 300 = _____   328 – 28 = _____

Count backward by tens.

890, 880, _____, _____, 850, _____, _____, 820, _____

Count backward by hundreds.

862, _____, 662, _____, _____, 362, _____, _____, 62

Write the number that is 10 less.

781 _____   85 _____   328 _____

Write the number that is 100 less.

528 _____   154 _____   350 _____

Final Test Chapters 1–5

Subtract.

881	803	746	202	236	318
− 17	− 29	− 48	− 96	− 48	− 45

802	438	877	602	930	738
− 359	− 118	− 335	− 420	− 115	− 309

118	813	946	145	918	226
− 71	− 320	− 439	− 91	− 110	− 14

925	408	770	789	967	571
− 666	− 121	− 162	− 601	− 18	− 101

Write the same number to complete each pair of equations.

☐ − 17 = 47	47 + 17 = ☐	308 − ☐ = 45	45 + ☐ = 308	51 − 47 = ☐	☐ + 47 = 51

☐ − 59 = 419	419 + 59 = ☐	337 − ☐ = 232	232 + ☐ = 337	☐ − 18 = 0	0 + 18 = ☐

Final Test Chapters 1–5

Measure each object. Tell how much longer one object is than the other.

 _____ cm

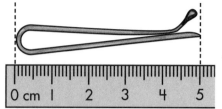 _____ cm

_____ cm longer

Write the money amounts. Subtract.

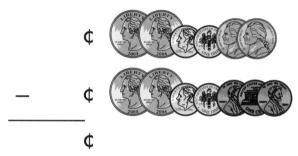

¢

— ¢

¢

Solve the problems.

Mr. Shaw bought 27 yards of fabric to make curtains.

Ms. Wolf bought 36 yards of fabric to make curtains.

How much more fabric did Ms. Wolf buy? _____ yards

A cone of popcorn cost 69¢.

Mia paid with 3 quarters.

How much change did Mia receive? _____ ¢

Blake earned 90¢ for taking out the trash.

He lent 25¢ to his little sister.

How much did Blake have left? _____ ¢

Scoring Record for Posttests, Mid-Test, and Final Test

Chapter Posttest	Your Score	Performance			
		Excellent	Very Good	Fair	Needs Improvement
1	____ of 41	41	37–41	29–36	28 or fewer
2	____ of 21	21	19–20	15–18	14 or fewer
3	____ of 18	18	16–18	13–15	12 or fewer
4	____ of 68	68	61–67	48–60	47 or fewer
5	____ of 27	27	24–26	19–23	18 or fewer
Mid-Test	____ of 82	82	74–81	57–73	56 or fewer
Final Test	____ of 127	127	114–126	89–113	88 or fewer

Record your test score in the Your Score column. See where your score falls in the Performance columns. If your score is fair or needs improvement, review the chapter material again.

Check What You Know
Subtraction Facts through 20

Subtract.

5 −4 = 1	14 −7 = 7	6 −4 = 2	10 −5 = 5	13 −5 = 8	18 −9 = 9
11 −4 = 7	19 −7 = 12	9 −6 = 3	4 −4 = 0	16 −8 = 8	15 −9 = 6
17 −8 = 9	8 −5 = 3	3 −0 = 3	20 −3 = 17	12 −4 = 8	7 −2 = 5
20 −7 = 13	9 −2 = 7	13 −8 = 5	7 −0 = 7	16 −5 = 11	11 −9 = 2
6 −5 = 1	15 −6 = 9	17 −7 = 10	4 −2 = 2	8 −3 = 5	19 −3 = 16
12 −2 = 10	5 −4 = 1	10 −7 = 3	18 −5 = 13	14 −6 = 8	3 −0 = 3

Check What You Know
Subtraction Facts through 20

SHOW YOUR WORK

Solve each problem.

The Jones family borrows 12 books from the library.

The Gomez family borrows 8 books.

How many more books does the Jones family borrow? __4__

There are 17 slices of pizza.

8 of them get eaten.

How many slices are left? __9__

20 students are in the library.

6 students leave.

How many students are still in the library? __14__

Sue borrows 12 books.

If Nina borrows 4 fewer books than Sue, how many books does Nina borrow? __8__

There are 18 desks on the first floor.

There are 7 desks on the second floor.

How many more desks are on the first floor? __11__

Lesson 1.1 Subtracting from 0 through 5

There are 4 fish. 2 swim away.
How many fish are left?

```
  4
− 2
  2  ← difference
```

Subtract.

4 −1 = 3	3 −3 = 0	1 −1 = 0	5 −4 = 1	3 −0 = 3	5 −2 = 3
2 −2 = 0	1 −0 = 1	5 −5 = 0	4 −3 = 1	5 −3 = 2	4 −0 = 4
2 −1 = 1	4 −2 = 2	2 −0 = 2	0 −0 = 0	3 −1 = 2	4 −1 = 3
2 −1 = 1	5 −0 = 5	4 −4 = 0	5 −2 = 3	2 −2 = 0	3 −3 = 0
3 −2 = 1	4 −1 = 3	5 −4 = 1	4 −2 = 2	3 −0 = 3	5 −1 = 4

Lesson 1.2 Subtracting from 6, 7, and 8

There are 7 balls.
5 are baseballs.
How many are not baseballs?

```
  7
− 5
  2
```

Subtract.

8 −4 = 4	7 −1 = 6	6 −3 = 3	7 −3 = 4	8 −5 = 3	6 −2 = 4
7 −0 = 7	8 −7 = 1	6 −4 = 2	7 −7 = 0	8 −3 = 5	6 −6 = 0
6 −1 = 5	8 −2 = 6	7 −4 = 3	6 −5 = 1	8 −6 = 2	7 −5 = 2
8 −8 = 0	6 −0 = 6	7 −2 = 5	8 −1 = 7	8 −0 = 8	7 −6 = 1
6 −2 = 4	8 −3 = 5	8 −4 = 4	7 −3 = 4	7 −7 = 0	6 −3 = 3

Lesson 1.3 Subtracting from 9 and 10

Dani has 10 postage stamps.   10

Felix has 6 postage stamps.   − 6

How many more stamps does Dani have?   4 ← difference

Subtract.

9 −6 = 3	10 −5 = 5	9 −3 = 6	10 −4 = 6	10 −9 = 1	9 −7 = 2
10 −1 = 9	9 −8 = 1	9 −5 = 4	10 −8 = 2	9 −1 = 8	10 −6 = 4
9 −0 = 9	9 −4 = 5	10 −7 = 3	9 −2 = 7	10 −3 = 7	10 −0 = 10
9 −9 = 0	10 −2 = 8	9 −3 = 6	10 −9 = 1	10 −1 = 9	9 −5 = 4
9 −8 = 1	10 −5 = 5	9 −1 = 8	9 −7 = 2	10 −8 = 2	10 −3 = 7

Lesson 1.4 Subtracting from 11, 12, and 13

13 = 1 ten 3 ones   Cross out to solve.   13 − 5 = 8

12 = 1 ten 2 ones   Cross out to solve.   12 − 7 = 5

Subtract.

12 −4 = 8	11 −9 = 2	13 −9 = 4	12 −5 = 7	13 −4 = 9	11 −6 = 5
11 −8 = 3	13 −6 = 7	13 −8 = 5	12 −3 = 9	11 −5 = 6	12 −6 = 6
13 −4 = 9	11 −7 = 4	12 −9 = 3	12 −4 = 8	13 −7 = 6	11 −3 = 8
12 −5 = 7	13 −5 = 8	12 −8 = 4	11 −5 = 6	11 −4 = 7	13 −9 = 4
11 −2 = 9	13 −6 = 7	11 −8 = 3	12 −3 = 9	12 −7 = 5	11 −6 = 5

Lesson 1.5 Subtracting from 14, 15, and 16

16 − 9 = 7   Think: 16 = 1 ten 6 ones

15 − 6 = 9   Cross out to solve. 15 = 1 ten 5 ones

Subtract.

14 −9 = 5	15 −8 = 7	16 −4 = 12	15 −3 = 12	14 −7 = 7	16 −0 = 16
14 −2 = 12	16 −7 = 9	14 −8 = 6	15 −5 = 10	16 −3 = 13	15 −2 = 13
14 −5 = 9	14 −3 = 11	15 −7 = 8	15 −0 = 15	16 −2 = 14	14 −6 = 8
14 −0 = 14	15 −1 = 14	15 −9 = 6	16 −8 = 8	15 −4 = 11	15 −6 = 9
16 −5 = 11	16 −9 = 7	16 −1 = 15	16 −2 = 14	14 −4 = 10	14 −1 = 13

Lesson 1.6 Subtracting from 17, 18, 19, and 20

17 − 9 = 8

Subtract.

18 −9 = 9	17 −3 = 14	20 −6 = 14	17 −9 = 8	19 −5 = 14	20 −9 = 11
18 −8 = 10	17 −8 = 9	19 −1 = 18	20 −8 = 12	17 −7 = 10	20 −3 = 17
18 −7 = 11	19 −9 = 10	18 −4 = 14	19 −7 = 12	18 −6 = 12	18 −2 = 16
17 −4 = 13	17 −5 = 12	20 −7 = 13	18 −3 = 15	19 −3 = 16	17 −2 = 15
20 −5 = 15	18 −1 = 17	17 −6 = 11	19 −8 = 11	20 −2 = 18	20 −10 = 10

Spectrum Subtraction
Grade 2

Answer Key

Lesson 1.7 Subtraction Practice

Complete the subtraction table. Subtract each number at the top from each number along the side. When you finish, look at the numbers you wrote. What patterns do you notice?

−	1	2	3	4	5	6	7	8	9
20	19	18	17	16	15	14	13	12	11
19	18	17	16	15	14	13	12	11	10
18	17	16	15	14	13	12	11	10	9
17	16	15	14	13	12	11	10	9	8
16	15	14	13	12	11	10	9	8	7
15	14	13	12	11	10	9	8	7	6
14	13	12	11	10	9	8	7	6	5
13	12	11	10	9	8	7	6	5	4
12	11	10	9	8	7	6	5	4	3
11	10	9	8	7	6	5	4	3	2
10	9	8	7	6	5	4	3	2	1
9	8	7	6	5	4	3	2	1	0
8	7	6	5	4	3	2	1	0	
7	6	5	4	3	2	1	0		
6	5	4	3	2	1	0			
5	4	3	2	1	0				
4	3	2	1	0					
3	2	1	0						
2	1	0							
1	0								

Spectrum Subtraction
Grade 2

Chapter 1, Lesson 7
Subtraction Facts through 20
13

Lesson 1.8 Problem Solving

SHOW YOUR WORK

Solve each problem.

Steve has 7 fish.
Ramon has 13 fish.
How many more fish does Ramon have? 6

$$\begin{array}{r} 13 \\ -\ 7 \\ \hline 6 \end{array}$$

Yolanda has 14 teddy bears.
Maria has 6 teddy bears.
How many more does Yolanda have? 8

$$\begin{array}{r} 14 \\ -\ 6 \\ \hline 8 \end{array}$$

Gina bakes 15 cupcakes.
Her friends eat 7.
How many cupcakes are left? 8

$$\begin{array}{r} 15 \\ -\ 7 \\ \hline 8 \end{array}$$

6 students were in the classroom at 9:00.
19 students were in the classroom at 10:00.
How many students came in between 9:00 and 10:00? 13

$$\begin{array}{r} 19 \\ -\ 6 \\ \hline 13 \end{array}$$

Mark has 18 toy cars.
He gives 9 away.
How many cars does he have left? 9

$$\begin{array}{r} 18 \\ -\ 9 \\ \hline 9 \end{array}$$

Spectrum Subtraction
Grade 2
14

Chapter 1, Lesson 8
Subtraction Facts through 20

Lesson 1.8 Problem Solving

SHOW YOUR WORK

Solve each problem.

Yoko picks 12 flowers.
She gives 6 to her mother.
How many flowers does Yoko have now? 6

$$\begin{array}{r} 12 \\ -\ 6 \\ \hline 6 \end{array}$$

Taylor has 20 books.
5 of them are about sports.
How many of them are not about sports? 15

$$\begin{array}{r} 20 \\ -\ 5 \\ \hline 15 \end{array}$$

Jesse mows 19 lawns.
Martin mows 7 lawns.
How many more lawns does Jesse mow? 12

$$\begin{array}{r} 19 \\ -\ 7 \\ \hline 12 \end{array}$$

Together, Kiki and Sara have 9 books.
Kiki has 5 books.
How many books does Sara have? 4

$$9 - 5 = \boxed{\ }$$

$$\begin{array}{r} 9 \\ -\ 5 \\ \hline 4 \end{array}$$

Spectrum Subtraction
Grade 2

Chapter 1, Lesson 8
Subtraction Facts through 20
15

Check What You Learned

Subtraction Facts through 20

CHAPTER 1 POSTTEST

Subtract.

$\begin{array}{r}13\\-4\\\hline9\end{array}$	$\begin{array}{r}7\\-1\\\hline6\end{array}$	$\begin{array}{r}4\\-2\\\hline2\end{array}$	$\begin{array}{r}14\\-8\\\hline6\end{array}$	$\begin{array}{r}10\\-9\\\hline1\end{array}$	$\begin{array}{r}5\\-0\\\hline5\end{array}$
$\begin{array}{r}19\\-9\\\hline10\end{array}$	$\begin{array}{r}15\\-6\\\hline9\end{array}$	$\begin{array}{r}6\\-6\\\hline0\end{array}$	$\begin{array}{r}17\\-8\\\hline9\end{array}$	$\begin{array}{r}8\\-2\\\hline6\end{array}$	$\begin{array}{r}12\\-6\\\hline6\end{array}$
$\begin{array}{r}16\\-8\\\hline8\end{array}$	$\begin{array}{r}18\\-9\\\hline9\end{array}$	$\begin{array}{r}20\\-4\\\hline16\end{array}$	$\begin{array}{r}3\\-3\\\hline0\end{array}$	$\begin{array}{r}11\\-8\\\hline3\end{array}$	$\begin{array}{r}9\\-9\\\hline0\end{array}$
$\begin{array}{r}20\\-8\\\hline12\end{array}$	$\begin{array}{r}10\\-6\\\hline4\end{array}$	$\begin{array}{r}12\\-4\\\hline8\end{array}$	$\begin{array}{r}3\\-1\\\hline2\end{array}$	$\begin{array}{r}16\\-9\\\hline7\end{array}$	$\begin{array}{r}7\\-5\\\hline2\end{array}$
$\begin{array}{r}18\\-3\\\hline15\end{array}$	$\begin{array}{r}9\\-2\\\hline7\end{array}$	$\begin{array}{r}11\\-7\\\hline4\end{array}$	$\begin{array}{r}15\\-9\\\hline6\end{array}$	$\begin{array}{r}6\\-3\\\hline3\end{array}$	$\begin{array}{r}13\\-5\\\hline8\end{array}$
$\begin{array}{r}4\\-0\\\hline4\end{array}$	$\begin{array}{r}14\\-5\\\hline9\end{array}$	$\begin{array}{r}2\\-1\\\hline1\end{array}$	$\begin{array}{r}17\\-6\\\hline11\end{array}$	$\begin{array}{r}19\\-5\\\hline14\end{array}$	$\begin{array}{r}8\\-4\\\hline4\end{array}$

Spectrum Subtraction
Grade 2
16

Check What You Learned
Chapter 1

 **Check What You Learned**   SHOW YOUR WORK

Subtraction Facts through 20

Solve each problem.

There are 15 bananas.

Joe takes 6.

How many bananas are left? _9_

The Changs picked 11 apples.

The next day, there were 3 apples left.

How many apples did the Changs eat? _8_

The store has 12 boxes of plums.

5 boxes of plums are sold.

How many boxes are left? _7_

Together, Grace and her sister bought 18 bananas.

Grace bought 9 bananas. $18 - \underline{9} = 9$

How many bananas did her sister buy? _9_

Mrs. Lopez has 19 hats.

3 of the hats have bows.

How many hats do not have bows? _16_

CHAPTER 2 PRETEST

Check What You Know

Subtracting 2-Digit Numbers (No Renaming)

Subtract.

46	77	63	19	35
−41	−50	−43	− 6	−13
5	27	20	13	22

57	88	97	29	48
−33	−61	−47	−12	−45
24	27	50	17	3

39	44	67	99	54
− 4	−13	−61	−79	−32
35	31	6	20	22

Solve each problem. $46 - \underline{22} = 24$

Mara saw 46. Then, some flew away.

Now, Mara sees only 24.

How many flew away? _22_

The store has 37.

It has 25. How many more does it have than _12_?

58 are on the field.

45 of the are playing soccer.

How many are not playing soccer? _13_

Lesson 2.1 Subtracting 2-Digit Numbers

		First, subtract the ones.	Then, subtract the tens.
77		77	77
−26		−26	−26
		1	51

Subtract.

49	87	36	54	68
−39	− 6	−24	−40	−16
10	81	12	14	52

79	78	42	19	26
−63	−25	−12	− 7	−11
16	53	30	12	15

59	28	95	74	67
−38	−14	−62	−50	−41
21	14	33	24	26

92	35	77	82	86
−81	− 5	−17	−51	−64
11	30	60	31	22

58	75	47	89	65
−53	−61	−37	−27	−60
5	14	10	62	5

Lesson 2.1 Subtracting 2-Digit Numbers

Subtract.

91	46	57	83	69
−80	−23	−32	−33	−55
11	23	25	50	14

34	48	73	56	76
−21	−22	−52	−23	−45
13	26	21	33	31

65	44	96	66	90
−13	−20	−85	−31	−70
52	24	11	35	20

43	72	88	94	29
−10	−30	−71	−84	− 5
33	42	17	10	24

99	18	26	86	38
− 8	− 4	−22	−55	−27
91	14	4	31	11

78	93	59	82	77
−64	− 3	−25	−50	−36
14	90	34	32	41

97	69	74	16	46
−72	− 8	−12	− 3	−35
25	61	62	13	11

Lesson 2.2 Subtraction Practice

Subtract. Use the tens blocks and ones blocks to help you.

66	47
− 31	− 16
35	31

78	19
− 27	− 12
51	7

66	94
− 26	− 30
40	64

52	26
− 11	− 13
41	13

NAME

Lesson 2.2 Subtraction Practice

Subtract.

67	54	73	99	68
− 45	− 20	− 63	− 83	− 62
22	34	10	16	6

79	88	37	66	89
− 7	− 70	− 34	− 6	− 44
72	18	3	60	45

57	95	47	87	49
− 32	− 63	− 4	− 42	− 48
25	32	43	45	1

65	76	85	92	38
− 30	− 33	− 31	− 52	− 17
35	43	54	40	21

96	43	58	93	84
− 81	− 11	− 7	− 53	− 71
15	32	51	40	13

94	63	29	97	61
− 14	− 3	− 15	− 23	− 40
80	60	14	74	21

49	24	77	98	45
− 6	− 4	− 51	− 80	− 23
43	20	26	18	22

NAME

Lesson 2.3 Problem Solving

SHOW YOUR WORK

Solve each problem.

Ms. Willis has 28 📖.
She returns 10 📖.
How many 📖 does Ms. Willis have left? 18

28
− 10
18

The first-grade class has 32 🧱.
The second-grade class has 30 🧱.
How many more 🧱 does the first-grade class have? 2

32
30
2

The art room has 65 🖊.
Students are using 22 🖊.
How many 🖊 are not being used? 43

65
22
43

Students had 44 🥛 at breakfast.
They had 59 🥛 at lunch. How many
more 🥛 did students have at lunch? 15

59
44
15

The library has 37 📖 about computers. 37 − 12 = ____
12 of the 📖 have been borrowed. How
many 📖 about computers are still in the library? 25

NAME

Lesson 2.3 Problem Solving

SHOW YOUR WORK

Solve each problem.

Cara has 35 ✏.
Ben has 39 ✏.
How many more ✏ does Ben have? 4

39
− 35
4

Marcus has 48 📮.
He uses 30 📮 to mail cards.
How many 📮 does he have left? 18

48
− 30
18

Pedro picks 39 🌸.
Jessica picks 28 🌸.
How many more 🌸 did Pedro pick? 11

39
− 28
11

There are 29 students with ⚽ or 🏈.
There are 9 students with 🏈.
How many students have ⚽? 20

29
− 9
20

Toya picks 48 🍎.
Jon picks 16 🍎.
How many more 🍎 than 🍏 do they have? 32

48
− 16
32

Check What You Learned

Subtracting 2-Digit Numbers (No Renaming)

Subtract.

79	44	68	52	85	26
− 63	− 20	− 55	− 11	− 35	− 4
16	24	13	41	50	22

99	76	19	45	76	39
− 46	− 6	− 16	− 12	− 42	− 15
53	70	3	33	34	24

77	64	95	37	29	96
− 4	− 54	− 70	− 7	− 12	− 52
73	10	25	30	17	44

Solve each problem.

Jermaine has 27 🥎. Brian has 31 🥎.
The boys lost 5 🥎 playing at the park.
How many total 🥎 do they have now? __53__

The class plants 35 🫘.
The 🫘 grow into 24 🪴. 3 of the 🪴 die.
How many 🪴 does the class have? __21__

Sydney makes 45 🧁.
Rosa makes 65 🧁.
How many more 🧁 does Rosa make? __20__

Spectrum Subtraction
Grade 2

Check What You Learned
Chapter 2
25

Check What You Know

Subtracting 2-Digit Numbers (With Renaming)

Subtract.

93	54	23	63	80
− 65	− 49	− 5	− 57	− 42
28	5	18	6	38

33	52	85	40	77
− 16	− 24	− 37	− 18	− 19
17	28	48	22	58

32	66	70	83	94
− 8	− 59	− 21	− 9	− 67
24	7	49	74	27

Solve each problem.

Anita picks 45 🍓.
She picks 61 🫐.
How many more 🫐 than 🍓 does she pick? __16__

Max's bucket holds 72 🍎.
Trey's bucket holds 44 🍎.
How many more 🍎 does Max's bucket hold? __28__

Carol and Paula have 91 🍓.   91 − 45 = 🍓
Paula picked 45 🍓.
How many 🍓 did Carol pick? __46__

Spectrum Subtraction
Grade 2
26

Check What You Know
Chapter 3

Lesson 3.1 Subtracting 2-Digit Numbers

		Rename 1 ten as 10 ones.	Subtract the ones.	Subtract the tens.
33 − 19	▦ = ▦▯	2 13 33 − 19	2 13 33 − 19 4	2 13 33 − 19 difference → 14
	3 tens 3 ones = 2 tens 13 ones			
60 − 28	▦ = ▦	5 10 60 − 28	5 10 60 − 28 2	5 10 60 − 28 difference → 32
	6 tens 0 ones = 5 tens 10 ones			

Subtract.

36	51	44	84	72
− 7	− 39	− 15	− 47	− 65
29	12	29	37	7

76	90	53	94	75
− 19	− 78	− 26	− 85	− 18
57	12	27	9	57

44	83	64	50	97
− 29	− 46	− 59	− 29	− 78
15	37	5	21	19

66	32	40	57	61
− 28	− 17	− 25	− 29	− 5
38	15	15	28	56

Spectrum Subtraction
Grade 2

Chapter 3, Lesson 1
Subtracting 2-Digit Numbers (With Renaming)
27

Lesson 3.1 Subtracting 2-Digit Numbers

	Rename 1 ten as 10 ones.	Subtract the ones.	Subtract the tens.
41 − 35	3 11 41 − 35	3 11 41 − 35 6	3 11 41 − 35 difference → 6
			Should you write a number in the tens place? __no__

Subtract.

72	28	66	96	82
− 69	− 19	− 48	− 8	− 37
3	9	18	88	45

80	24	60	54	91
− 67	− 8	− 43	− 45	− 55
13	16	17	9	36

42	82	92	77	81
− 38	− 56	− 63	− 68	− 33
4	26	29	9	48

74	86	73	95	30
− 58	− 48	− 49	− 87	− 14
16	38	24	8	16

46	31	71	22	96
− 27	− 23	− 34	− 6	− 69
19	8	37	16	27

Spectrum Subtraction
Grade 2
28

Chapter 3, Lesson 1
Subtracting 2-Digit Numbers (With Renaming)

Spectrum Subtraction
Grade 2

Answer Key

83

Lesson 3.2 Subtraction Practice

Use the regrouped tens blocks and ones blocks to help you subtract. Rename each crossed-out digit by writing a number in the box above. Then, solve the problem.

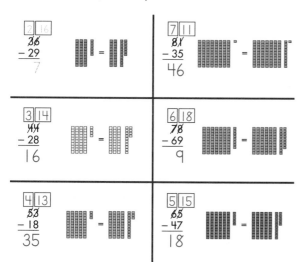

[2][16]		[7][11]	
3̸6̸	▥ ▥ = ▥	8̸1̸	
− 29		− 35	
7		46	

[3][14]		[6][18]	
4̸4̸	▥ = ▥	7̸8̸	
− 28		− 69	
16		9	

[4][13]		[5][15]	
5̸3̸	=	6̸5̸	
− 18		− 47	
35		18	

Lesson 3.2 Subtraction Practice

	Rename 1 ten as 10 ones.	Subtract the ones.	Subtract the tens.
51 − 23	4 11 5̸1̸ − 23	4 11 5̸1̸ − 23 8	4 11 5̸1̸ − 23 difference → 28

Subtract.

98	20	11	46	64
− 89	− 3	− 2	− 29	− 38
9	17	9	17	26
71	60	22	56	44
− 35	− 15	− 13	− 28	− 17
36	45	9	28	27
10	53	74	51	75
− 6	− 25	− 26	− 4	− 39
4	28	48	47	36
42	75	82	51	97
− 27	− 46	− 36	− 25	− 49
15	29	46	26	48
50	82	55	72	90
− 14	− 45	− 47	− 48	− 41
36	37	8	24	49
76	31	43	62	92
− 58	− 7	− 34	− 27	− 36
18	24	9	35	56

Lesson 3.3 Problem Solving

SHOW YOUR WORK

Solve each problem.

Marti catches 23 🐟 in the first pond.
She catches 14 🐟 in the second pond.
How many more 🐟 does
she catch in the first pond? __9__

1 13
2̸3̸
− 1 4
9

There are 42 🐦 in the tree.
There are 33 🐦 at the feeder.
How many more 🐦 are in the tree? __9__

42
− 33
9

Craig finds 13 🏆.
Zach finds 30 🏆.
How many more 🏆 does Zach find? __17__

30
− 13
17

There were 28 🐿 in the park. Some left.
There were 19 🐿 remaining in the park. 28 − __🐿__ = 19
How many 🐿 left the park? __9__

28 − 9 = 19

There are 32 🦢 in the barn.
There are 27 🦢 in the yard.
How many more 🦢 are in the barn? __5__

32
− 27
5

Lesson 3.3 Problem Solving

SHOW YOUR WORK

Solve each problem.

Freddie finds 33 🐌.
Tina finds 28 🐌.
How many more 🐌 does Freddie find? __5__

2 13
3̸3̸
− 2 8
5

Adam picks up 25 🐚 on Monday and 27 🐚 on Tuesday.
19 of the 🐚 are broken.
How many of the 🐚 are not broken? __33__

25   52
+ 27 − 19
52   33

Becky has 31 🥖.
She eats 8 🥖.
How many 🥖 does she have left? __23__

31
− 8
23

William has 26 🐭.   26 − __🐭__ = 18
He gives some 🐭 to a friend.
Now, he has only 18 🐭.
How many 🐭 did William give to his friend? __8__

26
− 8
18

Connie counts 42 🐟.
Annie counts 27 🐟.
How many more 🐟 does Connie count? __15__

42
− 27
15

Check What You Learned

Subtracting 2-Digit Numbers (With Renaming)

Subtract.

83	68	73	30	65
− 44	− 59	− 38	− 24	− 39
39	9	35	6	26

53	15	47	75	26
− 35	− 9	− 18	− 37	− 18
18	6	29	38	8

84	60	76	52	42
− 46	− 34	− 29	− 43	− 27
38	26	47	9	15

CHAPTER 3 POSTTEST

Solve each problem.

Ayisha buys 60 🍓.

51 of them are ripe.

How many of the 🍓 are not ripe? __9__

Nick picks 42 🍎.   42 − 18 = __🍎__

He sells 18 🍎 at the farm stand.

How many 🍎 does Nick have left? __24__

The farm stand sells 37 🎃 on Saturday

and 29 🎃 on Sunday. How many more

🎃 does it sell on Saturday? __8__

Mid-Test Chapters 1–3

Subtract.

5	11	15	13	17	8
− 3	− 4	− 5	− 5	− 3	− 1
2	7	10	8	14	7

3	13	19	6	16	13
− 1	− 6	− 6	− 4	− 3	− 1
2	7	13	2	13	12

4	5	7	17	14	9
− 1	− 4	− 6	− 4	− 1	− 6
3	1	1	13	13	3

17	3	18	17	10	6
− 2	− 2	− 2	− 8	− 1	− 2
15	1	16	9	9	4

12	11	17	18	20	6
− 9	− 5	− 1	− 6	− 4	− 5
3	6	16	12	16	1

11	15	9	8	9	5
− 1	− 4	− 4	− 2	− 2	− 2
10	11	5	6	7	3

CHAPTERS 1–3 MID-TEST

Mid-Test Chapters 1–3

SHOW YOUR WORK

Solve each problem.

There are 20 🧢.

There are 8 👒.

How many more 🧢? __12__

20
− 8
12

There are 12 🥄 on the table.

There are 6 🥄 in the drawer.

How many more 🥄 are on the table? __6__

12
− 6
6

There are 18 🍎.

We eat 9 🍎.

How many 🍎 are left? __9__

18
− 9
9

There are 16 🦁 under a tree.

9 🦁 walk away.

How many 🦁 are left? __7__

16
− 9
7

Tanya has 11 🌷.

Curtis has 7 🌷.

How many more 🌷 does Tanya have? __4__

11
− 7
4

CHAPTERS 1–3 MID-TEST

Mid-Test Chapters 1–3

Subtract.

97	98	60	65	74	76
− 91	− 13	− 31	− 50	− 37	− 46
6	85	29	15	37	30

46	64	72	86	97	36
− 35	− 56	− 34	− 54	− 66	− 32
11	8	38	32	31	4

65	99	55	70	78	84
− 24	− 11	− 38	− 42	− 55	− 37
41	88	17	28	23	47

94	65	71	37	88	85
− 38	− 16	− 35	− 17	− 20	− 59
56	49	36	20	68	26

53	75	95	92	66	35
− 45	− 61	− 39	− 46	− 9	− 21
8	14	56	46	57	14

88	50	52	69	90	66
− 60	− 14	− 28	− 42	− 45	− 56
28	36	24	27	45	10

CHAPTERS 1–3 MID-TEST

Mid-Test Chapters 1–3

SHOW YOUR WORK

Solve each problem.

Emil has 63 📖.
He lends 11 📖 to Jeff.
How many 📖 does Emil have left? __52__

$$\begin{array}{r} 63 \\ -11 \\ \hline 52 \end{array}$$

Terrence has 24 📖.
Bella has 91 📖.
How many more 📖 does Bella have? __67__

$$\begin{array}{r} 91 \\ -24 \\ \hline 67 \end{array}$$

An apple costs 90¢.
An orange costs 75¢.
How much more does an apple cost? __15__ ¢

$$\begin{array}{r} 90 \\ -75 \\ \hline 15 \end{array}$$

The earth club plants 86 🌳 on Saturday
and 53 🌳 on Sunday.
How many more 🌳 did they plant on Saturday? __33__

$$\begin{array}{r} 86 \\ -53 \\ \hline 33 \end{array}$$

The earth club plants 45 🌻.
24 of the 🌻 are red. 13 of the 🌻 are yellow.
How many 🌻 are not red or yellow? __8__

$$\begin{array}{r} 24 \\ +13 \\ \hline 37 \end{array} \qquad \begin{array}{r} 45 \\ -37 \\ \hline 8 \end{array}$$

CHAPTERS 1-3 MID-TEST

CHAPTER 4 PRETEST

Check What You Know

Subtracting from 3-Digit Numbers

Write the number shown by the blocks. Then, use the blocks to help you solve the subtraction problems.

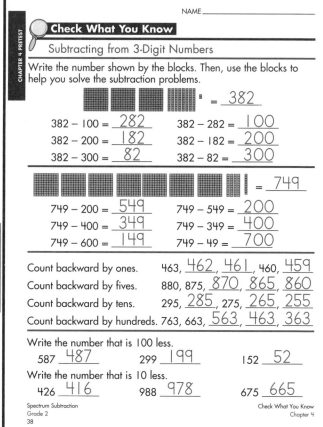 = __382__

382 – 100 = __282__   382 – 282 = __100__
382 – 200 = __182__   382 – 182 = __200__
382 – 300 = __82__   382 – 82 = __300__

= __749__

749 – 200 = __549__   749 – 549 = __200__
749 – 400 = __349__   749 – 349 = __400__
749 – 600 = __149__   749 – 49 = __700__

Count backward by ones.   463, __462__, __461__, 460, __459__
Count backward by fives.   880, 875, __870__, __865__, __860__
Count backward by tens.   295, __285__, 275, __265__, __255__
Count backward by hundreds. 763, 663, __563__, __463__, __363__

Write the number that is 100 less.
587 __487__   299 __199__   152 __52__

Write the number that is 10 less.
426 __416__   988 __978__   675 __665__

Check What You Know

Subtracting from 3-Digit Numbers

CHAPTER 4 PRETEST

Subtract.

123 – 15 **108**	87 – 23 **64**	545 – 35 **510**	79 – 63 **16**	187 – 93 **94**	782 – 143 **639**
898 – 454 **444**	763 – 321 **442**	981 – 133 **848**	725 – 125 **600**	805 – 73 **732**	120 – 80 **40**
76 – 41 **35**	87 – 35 **52**	72 – 35 **37**	153 – 92 **61**	763 – 154 **609**	876 – 450 **426**
138 – 52 **86**	192 – 175 **17**	712 – 92 **620**	392 – 286 **106**	510 – 347 **163**	692 – 486 **206**
120 – 45 **75**	198 – 79 **119**	175 – 84 **91**	908 – 67 **841**	798 – 104 **694**	586 – 62 **524**
573 – 110 **463**	278 – 178 **100**	779 – 66 **713**	741 – 514 **227**	944 – 345 **599**	525 – 430 **95**

Lesson 4.1 Using Place Value 150 through 199

Use the hundreds, tens, and ones blocks to help you solve the subtraction problems.

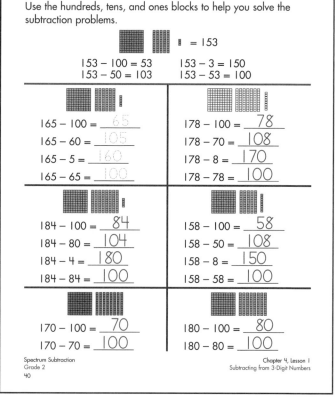 = 153

153 – 100 = 53   153 – 3 = 150
153 – 50 = 103   153 – 53 = 100

165 – 100 = __65__
165 – 60 = __105__
165 – 5 = __160__
165 – 65 = __100__

178 – 100 = __78__
178 – 70 = __108__
178 – 8 = __170__
178 – 78 = __100__

184 – 100 = __84__
184 – 80 = __104__
184 – 4 = __180__
184 – 84 = __100__

158 – 100 = __58__
158 – 50 = __108__
158 – 8 = __150__
158 – 58 = __100__

170 – 100 = __70__
170 – 70 = __100__

180 – 100 = __80__
180 – 80 = __100__

Spectrum Subtraction
Grade 2

86

Answer Key

Lesson 4.2 Using Place Value 200 through 399

Use the hundreds, tens, and ones blocks to help you solve the subtraction problems.

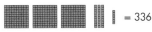 = 336

336 − 100 = 236   336 − 236 = 100
336 − 200 = 136   336 − 136 = 200
336 − 300 = 36   336 − 36 = 300

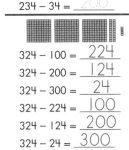

234 − 100 = 134
234 − 200 = 34
234 − 134 = 100
234 − 34 = 200

289 − 100 = 189
289 − 200 = 89
289 − 189 = 100
289 − 89 = 200

324 − 100 = 224
324 − 200 = 124
324 − 300 = 24
324 − 224 = 100
324 − 124 = 200
324 − 24 = 300

341 − 100 = 241
341 − 200 = 141
341 − 300 = 41
341 − 241 = 100
341 − 141 = 200
341 − 41 = 300

Lesson 4.3 Using Place Value 400 through 699

Use the hundreds, tens, and ones blocks to help you solve the subtraction problems.

 = 647

647 − 100 = 547   647 − 447 = 200
647 − 300 = 347   647 − 247 = 400
647 − 500 = 147   647 − 47 = 600

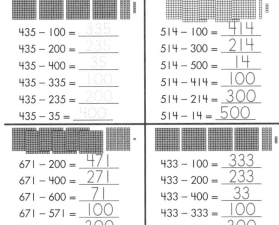

435 − 100 = 335
435 − 200 = 235
435 − 400 = 35
435 − 335 = 100
435 − 235 = 200
435 − 35 = 400

514 − 100 = 414
514 − 300 = 214
514 − 500 = 14
514 − 414 = 100
514 − 214 = 300
514 − 14 = 500

671 − 200 = 471
671 − 400 = 271
671 − 600 = 71
671 − 571 = 100
671 − 371 = 300
671 − 71 = 600

433 − 100 = 333
433 − 200 = 233
433 − 400 = 33
433 − 333 = 100
433 − 133 = 300
433 − 33 = 400

Lesson 4.4 Using Place Value 700 through 999

Use the hundreds, tens, and ones blocks to help you solve the subtraction problems.

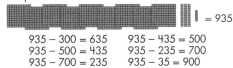 = 935

935 − 300 = 635   935 − 435 = 500
935 − 500 = 435   935 − 235 = 700
935 − 700 = 235   935 − 35 = 900

722 − 200 = _____   722 − 322 = _____
722 − 400 = _____   722 − 122 = _____
722 − 600 = _____   722 − 22 = _____

956 − 300 = 656   956 − 456 = 500
956 − 600 = 356   956 − 256 = 700
956 − 900 = 56   956 − 56 = 900

843 − 300 = 543   843 − 343 = 500
843 − 500 = 343   843 − 243 = 600
843 − 700 = 143   843 − 43 = 800

Lesson 4.5 Skip Counting Back

Count backward by ones.

317, 316, 315, 314, 313, 312, 311, 310

422, 421, 420, 419, 418, 417, 416, 415

Count backward by fives.

635, 630, 625, 620, 615, 610, 605 600

820, 815, 810, 805, 800, 795, 790, 785

475, 470, 465, 460, 455, 450, 445, 440

Count backward by tens.

650, 640, 630 620, 610, 600, 590, 580

700, 690, 680, 670, 660, 650, 640, 630

320, 310, 300, 290, 280, 270, 260, 250

Count backward by hundreds.

700, 600, 500, 400, 300, 200, 100, 0

900, 800, 700, 600, 500, 400, 300, 200

800, 700, 600, 500, 400, 300, 200, 100

NAME _____

Lesson 4.5 Skip Counting Back

Count backward by hundreds. Start at 950.

950, _850_, 750, _650_, _550_, 450, _350_

Count backward by ones. Start at 773.

773, 772, 771, _770_, _769_, _768_, _767_

Count backward by tens. Start at 435.

435, 425, _415_, _405_, 395, _385_, _375_

Count backward by hundreds. Start at 827.

827, 727, _627_, _527_, 427, _327_, _227_

Count backward by fives. Start at 185.

185, _180_, _175_, _170_, _165_, 160, 155

Count backward by ones. Start at 999.

999, 998, 997, _996_, _995_, _994_, _993_

Count backward by fives. Start at 300.

300, 295, _290_, _285_, 280, _275_, _270_

Count backward by tens. Start at 610.

610, _600_, 590, _580_, _570_, 560, _550_

NAME _____

Lesson 4.6 Mentally Subtract 100

When you subtract 100 from a three-digit number, only the number in the hundreds place changes. It is one less. The numbers in the tens and ones places stay the same.

$$654 - 100 = 554$$
$$6 - 1 = 5$$

Subtract 100 from each number. Solve the problem only in your mind. Write the number in the thought bubble.

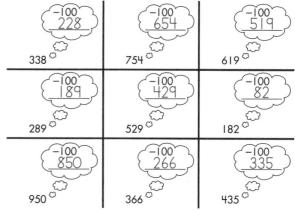

−100 228	−100 654	−100 519
338	754	619
−100 189	−100 429	−100 82
289	529	182
−100 850	−100 266	−100 335
950	366	435

NAME _____

Lesson 4.7 Mentally Subtract 10

When you subtract 10 from a three-digit number, only the number in the tens place changes. It is one less. The numbers in the hundreds and ones places stay the same.

$$382 - 10 = 372$$
$$8 - 1 = 7$$

Subtract 10 from each number. Solve the problem only in your mind. Write the number in the thought bubble.

−10 328	−10 744	−10 609
338	754	619
−10 279	−10 519	−10 172
289	529	182
−10 940	−10 356	−10 425
950	366	435

NAME _____

Lesson 4.8 Subtracting 2 Digits from 3 Digits

| Subtract the ones. | To subtract the tens, rename the 1 hundred and 2 tens as 12 tens. | Subtract the tens. | |
| 125 − 84 | 125 − 84 = 1 | 1̸2̸5 (12) − 84 = 1 | 1̸2̸5 (12) − 84 = 41 | minuend subtrahend difference |

Subtract.

113 − 33 = 80	121 − 60 = 61	195 − 44 = 151	122 − 11 = 111	147 − 53 = 94
143 − 62 = 81	180 − 70 = 110	119 − 15 = 104	123 − 12 = 111	186 − 65 = 121
154 − 13 = 141	127 − 83 = 44	187 − 67 = 120	135 − 42 = 93	115 − 24 = 91
132 − 51 = 81	177 − 43 = 134	192 − 71 = 121	186 − 92 = 94	134 − 72 = 62
129 − 86 = 43	176 − 75 = 101	120 − 40 = 80	194 − 53 = 141	189 − 62 = 127

Lesson 4.8 Subtracting 2 Digits from 3 Digits

Rename 5 tens and 3 ones as 4 tens and 13 ones.	Subtract the ones.	Rename 1 hundred and 4 tens as 14 tens.	Subtract the tens.	
153 − 65	1⁴5̶3̶¹³ − 65	1⁴5̶3̶¹³ − 65 8	¹⁴1̶5̶3̶¹³ − 65 8	¹⁴1̶5̶3̶¹³ minuend − 65 subtrahend 88 difference

Subtract.

162 − 73 89	175 − 97 78	182 − 94 88	103 − 17 86	116 − 39 77
174 − 95 79	147 − 68 79	132 − 65 67	115 − 49 66	107 − 39 68
101 − 75 26	100 − 92 8	127 − 79 48	133 − 44 89	142 − 73 69
141 − 63 78	137 − 79 58	142 − 73 69	153 − 67 86	155 − 96 59
100 − 72 28	106 − 48 58	117 − 88 29	124 − 66 58	163 − 89 74

Lesson 4.9 Subtraction Practice

Subtract.

132 − 71 61	196 − 87 109	165 − 59 106	163 − 71 92	119 − 29 90
106 − 51 55	100 − 29 71	153 − 69 84	147 − 88 59	192 − 75 117
175 − 95 80	169 − 99 70	142 − 37 105	140 − 93 47	131 − 57 74
167 − 76 91	173 − 82 91	192 − 95 97	143 − 77 66	126 − 54 72
117 − 26 91	100 − 33 67	175 − 46 129	142 − 57 85	136 − 47 89

Lesson 4.9 Subtraction Practice

Subtract.

144 − 86 58	122 − 31 91	191 − 75 116	175 − 93 82	144 − 65 79
121 − 37 84	106 − 42 64	165 − 43 122	162 − 47 115	181 − 57 124
106 − 99 7	127 − 49 78	136 − 58 78	124 − 75 49	143 − 52 91
685 − 96 589	444 − 67 377	612 − 22 590	786 − 19 767	950 − 99 851
865 − 92 773	710 − 7 703	475 − 89 386	627 − 10 617	751 − 93 658
509 − 75 434	696 − 5 691	815 − 25 790	545 − 57 488	115 − 72 43

Lesson 4.10 Subtracting 3-Digit Numbers

Rename 2 tens and 1 one as 1 ten and 11 ones. Then, subtract the ones.	Rename 6 hundreds and 1 ten as 5 hundreds and 11 tens. Then, subtract the tens.	Subtract the hundreds.	
621 −259	6̶2̶1̶¹¹¹ −259 2	5̶6̶2̶1̶¹¹ −259 62	5̶6̶2̶1̶¹¹ minuend −259 subtrahend 362 difference

Subtract.

321 −109 212	745 −152 593	639 −150 489	830 −710 120	626 −146 480
729 −321 408	657 −451 206	386 −107 279	411 −305 106	486 −109 377
983 −652 331	971 −572 399	876 −357 519	549 −360 189	721 −144 577
256 −142 114	347 −139 208	725 −196 529	863 −692 171	980 −532 448

Lesson 4.10 Subtracting 3-Digit Numbers

Rename 1 ten and 3 ones as 0 tens and 13 ones. Then, subtract the ones.	Rename 5 hundreds and 0 tens as 4 hundreds and 10 tens. Then, subtract the tens.	Subtract the hundreds.

$$\begin{array}{r} 513 \\ -125 \\ \hline \end{array} \qquad \begin{array}{r} 0\,13 \\ 5\cancel{1}\cancel{3} \\ -125 \\ \hline 8 \end{array} \qquad \begin{array}{r} 10 \\ 4\,\cancel{0}\,13 \\ \cancel{5}\cancel{1}\cancel{3} \\ -125 \\ \hline 88 \end{array} \qquad \begin{array}{r} 10 \\ 4\,\cancel{0}\,13 \\ \cancel{5}\cancel{1}\cancel{3} \\ -125 \\ \hline 388 \end{array}$$

minuend
subtrahend
difference

Subtract.

543 −457 = **86**	762 −135 = **627**	132 −107 = **25**	921 −571 = **350**	631 −545 = **86**
531 −250 = **281**	720 −371 = **349**	582 −357 = **225**	793 −457 = **336**	612 −483 = **129**
543 −206 = **337**	432 −257 = **175**	710 −512 = **198**	432 −119 = **313**	186 −107 = **79**
712 −347 = **365**	690 −320 = **370**	451 −253 = **198**	512 −308 = **204**	861 −172 = **689**

Lesson 4.11 Subtraction Practice

Subtract.

142 −131 = **11**	192 −127 = **65**	543 −121 = **422**	192 −154 = **38**	190 −150 = **40**
182 −159 = **23**	396 −185 = **211**	540 −375 = **165**	513 −211 = **302**	312 −192 = **120**
412 −306 = **106**	790 −205 = **585**	674 −556 = **118**	700 −310 = **390**	690 −541 = **149**
898 −844 = **54**	412 −340 = **72**	775 −436 = **339**	962 −841 = **121**	829 −394 = **435**
796 −318 = **478**	710 −696 = **14**	971 −320 = **651**	583 −421 = **162**	710 −190 = **520**

Lesson 4.11 Subtraction Practice

Subtract.

711 −547 = **164**	786 −457 = **329**	210 −102 = **108**	232 −144 = **88**	457 −310 = **147**
740 −310 = **430**	862 −456 = **406**	610 −232 = **378**	695 −159 = **536**	869 −341 = **528**
934 −281 = **653**	752 −557 = **195**	745 −494 = **251**	658 −237 = **421**	674 −164 = **510**
868 −256 = **612**	430 −253 = **177**	580 −371 = **209**	853 −359 = **494**	797 −191 = **606**
711 −278 = **433**	721 −135 = **586**	864 −724 = **140**	935 −691 = **244**	722 −429 = **293**

💡 Check What You Learned

Subtracting from 3-Digit Numbers

CHAPTER 4 POSTTEST

Write the number shown by the blocks. Then, use the blocks to help you solve the subtraction problems.

 = **568**

568 − 200 = **368**	568 − 368 = **200**
568 − 400 = **168**	568 − 168 = **400**
568 − 500 = **68**	568 − 68 = **500**

= **906**

906 − 300 = **606**	906 − 706 = **200**
906 − 600 = **306**	906 − 506 = **400**
906 − 900 = **6**	906 − 6 = **900**

Count backward by ones. 111, **110**, **109**, 108, **107**

Count backward by fives. 660, 655, **650**, **645**, **640**

Count backward by tens. 394, **384**, 374, **364**, **354**

Count backward by hundreds. 855, 755, **655**, **555**, **455**

Write the number that is 100 less.
850 **750**   172 **72**   549 **449**

Write the number that is 10 less.
822 **812**   395 **385**   412 **402**

Check What You Learned
Subtracting from 3-Digit Numbers

Subtract.

172 − 35 **137**	192 − 86 **106**	174 − 96 **78**	120 − 80 **40**	310 − 40 **270**	293 −107 **186**
986 −698 **288**	862 −245 **617**	352 −121 **231**	187 − 72 **115**	647 −253 **394**	547 −183 **364**
662 −503 **159**	708 −231 **477**	456 −269 **187**	882 −199 **683**	753 −268 **485**	712 −543 **169**
185 −153 **32**	216 − 53 **163**	156 − 40 **116**	687 −246 **441**	923 −814 **109**	824 −487 **337**
905 − 26 **879**	688 −141 **547**	648 −141 **507**	906 − 27 **879**	648 −597 **51**	916 −411 **505**
793 −144 **649**	643 −508 **135**	997 −398 **599**	852 −399 **453**	158 − 63 **95**	250 −136 **114**

CHAPTER 4 POSTTEST

Check What You Know
Using Subtraction

CHAPTER 5 PRETEST

Subtract. Check each answer by writing an addition problem. The first one is done for you.

126 − 74 **52** **+ 74** **126**	86 − 17 **69** + 17 **86**	542 −150 **392** +150 **542**	960 − 26 **934** + 26 **960**	97 − 82 **15** + 82 **97**
512 − 18 **494** + 18 **512**	20 − 16 **4** + 16 **20**	488 −199 **289** +199 **488**	49 − 25 **24** + 25 **49**	614 −276 **338** +276 **614**

Write the missing number in each equation.

99 − **54** 45	487 −256 **231**	156 − **25** 131	**773** − 58 715
635 − **535** 100	**452** − 52 400	816 −620 **196**	422 − **0** 422

Check What You Know
Using Subtraction

CHAPTER 5 PRETEST

Measure each object. Tell how much longer one object is than the other.

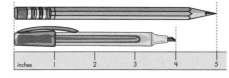

5 inches

4 inches

1 inch longer

Write the money amounts. Subtract.

58¢ − 16¢ **42¢**	88¢ − 69¢ **19¢**

Solve the problems.

Marco's bean plant grew to 16 inches tall.

Julisa's bean plant grew to 21 inches tall.

How much taller is Julisa's plant? **5** inches

Sydney found 2 quarters, 1 nickel, and 3 pennies.

She bought a cup of lemonade for 45¢

How much money did she have left? **13** ¢

Lesson 5.1 Checking Subtraction with Addition

To check
982 − 657 = 325,
add 657 to 325.

982
−657
325
+657
982

These should be the same.

Subtract. Check each answer.

720 −150 **570** **+150** **720**	321 − 83 **238** + 83 **321**	125 − 92 **33** + 92 **125**	983 −657 **326** +657 **983**	456 −291 **165** +291 **456**
300 −179 **121** +179 **300**	119 −104 **15** +104 **119**	423 −197 **226** +197 **423**	259 −147 **112** +147 **259**	592 −463 **129** +463 **592**
519 −120 **399** +120 **519**	540 −320 **220** +320 **540**	192 − 86 **106** + 86 **192**	710 −447 **263** +447 **710**	683 −419 **264** +419 **683**
719 −532 **187** +532 **719**	919 −457 **462** +457 **919**	687 −250 **437** +250 **687**	912 −609 **303** +609 **912**	542 −327 **215** +327 **542**

Lesson 5.2 Checking Addition with Subtraction

To check
215 + 109 = 324,
subtract 109 from 324.

```
    2 1 5  ⌐ ⌐ ⌐ ⌐
  + 1 0 9         ¦
  ─────          ¦   These should be the same.
    3 2 4         ¦
  - 1 0 9         ¦
  ─────          ¦
    2 1 5  ← ─ ─ ┘
```

Add. Check each answer.

```
  1 5 7      7 1 9      3 1 2      2 1 3      3 0 6
+ 2 1 2    + 1 8 2    + 1 0 5    + 5 1 9    + 2 1 5
─────      ─────      ─────      ─────      ─────
  3 6 9      9 0 1      4 1 7      7 3 2      5 2 1
- 2 1 2    - 1 8 2    - 1 0 5    - 5 1 9    - 2 1 5
─────      ─────      ─────      ─────      ─────
  1 5 7      7 1 9      3 1 2      2 1 3      3 0 6
```

```
  7 1 0      3 5 7      7 1 2      6 1 4      3 1 2
+ 2 1 8    + 2 4 9    + 2 6 3    + 2 9 1    +   8 5
─────      ─────      ─────      ─────      ─────
  9 2 8      6 0 6      9 7 5      9 0 5      3 9 7
- 2 1 8    - 2 4 9    - 2 6 3    - 2 9 1    -   8 5
─────      ─────      ─────      ─────      ─────
  7 1 0      3 5 7      7 1 2      6 1 4      3 1 2
```

```
  3 0 0      5 9 1      6 1 2      4 2 5      4 1 1
+ 5 4 7    + 1 2 0    + 3 1 9    + 1 2 5    + 1 2 0
─────      ─────      ─────      ─────      ─────
  8 4 7      7 1 1      9 3 1      5 5 0      5 3 1
- 5 4 7    - 1 2 0    - 3 1 9    - 1 2 5    - 1 2 0
─────      ─────      ─────      ─────      ─────
  3 0 0      5 9 1      6 1 2      4 2 5      4 1 1
```

```
  8 6 3      4 5 9      6 0 3      7 1 1      2 5 2
+   9 2    + 1 3 0    + 2 0 9    + 1 9 1    + 1 3 0
─────      ─────      ─────      ─────      ─────
  9 5 5      5 8 9      8 1 2      9 0 2      3 8 2
-   9 2    - 1 3 0    - 2 0 9    - 1 9 1    - 1 3 0
─────      ─────      ─────      ─────      ─────
  8 6 3      4 5 9      6 0 3      7 1 1      2 5 2
```

Lesson 5.3 Finding an Unknown Number

Use subtraction and addition to find the missing number in each equation. Write the missing number in the box.

```
  [20]       1 0 0       1 6 3       [775]
-   7      - [37]     - [34]      -  5 2
─────      ─────      ─────       ─────
  1 3         6 3       1 2 9       7 2 3
```

```
  1 4 4       9 9 6       [158]       7 9
-  [0]      - 3 8 0     -  5 8     - [2]
─────      ─────       ─────       ─────
  1 4 4      [616]       1 0 0       7 7
```

```
  2 2 6       [999]       7 8 3       [216]
- 1 9 5     -  9 9     - [233]     -  8 4
─────       ─────      ─────       ─────
  [31]        9 0 0       5 5 0       1 3 2
```

```
    6 5       [100]        5 5       [414]
-    9      -  1 0      -  [6]     - 1 3 3
─────       ─────       ─────      ─────
  [56]         9 0         4 9       2 8 1
```

Lesson 5.3 Finding an Unknown Number

In each equation, a symbol stands for a missing number. Write the missing number beside the symbol at the bottom of the page.

88 – ✳ = 76   622 – ✚ = 254

458 – ♥ = 451   ✳ – 12 = 0

86 – 86 = ◉   ☺ – 33 = 966

200 – ϟ = 171   778 – ◉ = 778

100 – 93 = ♥   100 – ϟ = 71

★ – 13 = 37   ▲ – 95 = 104

220 – ▲ = 21   800 – ★ = 750

☺ – 700 = 299   ✚ – 81 = 287

▲ 199   ✳ 12   ♥ 7

★ 50   ☺ 999   ✚ 368

ϟ 29   ◉ 0

Lesson 5.4 How Much Longer?

Measure each object. Tell how much longer one object is than the other.

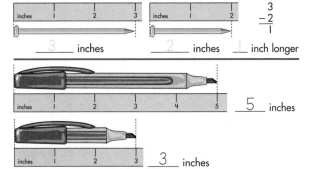

```
    3
  - 2
  ───
    1
```

_3_ inches   _2_ inches   _1_ inch longer

_5_ inches

_3_ inches

_2_ inches longer

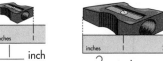

_1_ inch   _2_ inches   _1_ inch longer

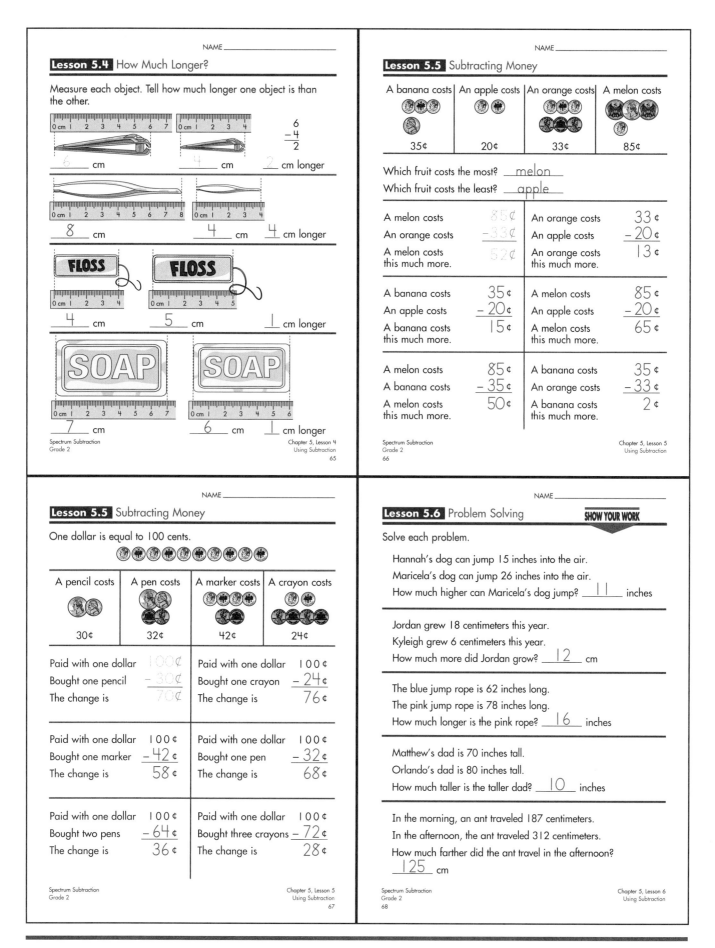

Lesson 5.4 How Much Longer?

Measure each object. Tell how much longer one object is than the other.

$$\begin{array}{r} 6 \\ -4 \\ \hline 2 \end{array}$$

__6__ cm   __4__ cm   __2__ cm longer

__8__ cm   __4__ cm   __4__ cm longer

FLOSS   FLOSS

__4__ cm   __5__ cm   __1__ cm longer

SOAP   SOAP

__7__ cm   __6__ cm   __1__ cm longer

Spectrum Subtraction
Grade 2

Chapter 5, Lesson 4
Using Subtraction
65

Lesson 5.5 Subtracting Money

A banana costs	An apple costs	An orange costs	A melon costs
35¢	20¢	33¢	85¢

Which fruit costs the most? __melon__

Which fruit costs the least? __apple__

A melon costs	85¢	An orange costs	33¢
An orange costs	−33¢	An apple costs	−20¢
A melon costs this much more.	52¢	An orange costs this much more.	13¢
A banana costs	35¢	A melon costs	85¢
An apple costs	−20¢	An apple costs	−20¢
A banana costs this much more.	15¢	A melon costs this much more.	65¢
A melon costs	85¢	A banana costs	35¢
A banana costs	−35¢	An orange costs	−33¢
A melon costs this much more.	50¢	A banana costs this much more.	2¢

Spectrum Subtraction
Grade 2
66

Chapter 5, Lesson 5
Using Subtraction

Lesson 5.5 Subtracting Money

One dollar is equal to 100 cents.

A pencil costs	A pen costs	A marker costs	A crayon costs
30¢	32¢	42¢	24¢

Paid with one dollar	100¢	Paid with one dollar	100¢
Bought one pencil	−30¢	Bought one crayon	−24¢
The change is	70¢	The change is	76¢
Paid with one dollar	100¢	Paid with one dollar	100¢
Bought one marker	−42¢	Bought one pen	−32¢
The change is	58¢	The change is	68¢
Paid with one dollar	100¢	Paid with one dollar	100¢
Bought two pens	−64¢	Bought three crayons	−72¢
The change is	36¢	The change is	28¢

Spectrum Subtraction
Grade 2

Chapter 5, Lesson 5
Using Subtraction
67

Lesson 5.6 Problem Solving   **SHOW YOUR WORK**

Solve each problem.

Hannah's dog can jump 15 inches into the air.
Maricela's dog can jump 26 inches into the air.
How much higher can Maricela's dog jump? __11__ inches

Jordan grew 18 centimeters this year.
Kyleigh grew 6 centimeters this year.
How much more did Jordan grow? __12__ cm

The blue jump rope is 62 inches long.
The pink jump rope is 78 inches long.
How much longer is the pink rope? __16__ inches

Matthew's dad is 70 inches tall.
Orlando's dad is 80 inches tall.
How much taller is the taller dad? __10__ inches

In the morning, an ant traveled 187 centimeters.
In the afternoon, the ant traveled 312 centimeters.
How much farther did the ant travel in the afternoon?
__125__ cm

Spectrum Subtraction
Grade 2
68

Chapter 5, Lesson 6
Using Subtraction

Spectrum Subtraction
Grade 2

Answer Key

Lesson 5.6 Problem Solving   **SHOW YOUR WORK**

Solve each problem.

At a food stand, a bean burrito costs 99¢

A soft chicken taco costs 79¢

How much more is the burrito? __20__ ¢

Caleb had three quarters in his pocket.

He bought a postcard for 36¢

How much money does he have left? __39__ ¢

Bonnie has two dimes and six pennies.

At the carnival, she wants to buy a ticket for 25¢

Does Bonnie have enough money? __yes__

Dad gave Roland one dollar.

Roland will spend half of the money and save the other half.

How much will Roland save? __50__ ¢

Cassie's mother gave her money to spend at the book fair: 1 dollar bill, 2 quarters, 4 dimes, 1 nickel, and 5 pennies.

Cassie wants to buy a book that costs 3 dollars.

Does Cassie have enough money? __no__

Spectrum Subtraction
Grade 2

Chapter 5, Lesson 6
Using Subtraction
69

Check What You Learned

Using Subtraction

Subtract. Check each answer by writing an addition problem. The first one is done for you.

CHAPTER 5 POSTTEST

86	508	52	171	300
− 9	− 99	− 6	− 55	− 42
77	409	46	116	258
+ 9	+ 99	+ 6	+ 55	+ 42
86	508	52	171	300

53	256	629	87	711
−17	−188	− 29	− 4	−276
36	68	600	83	435
+17	+188	+ 29	+ 4	+276
53	256	629	87	711

Write the missing number in each equation.

802	480	99	300
− 677	−315	− 91	− 72
125	165	8	228

456	690	100	809
− 375	− 52	− 58	− 109
81	638	42	700

Spectrum Subtraction
Grade 2
70

Check What You Learned
Chapter 5

Check What You Learned

Using Subtraction

Measure each object. Tell how much longer one object is than the other.

14	cm
11	cm
3	cm longer

CHAPTER 5 POSTTEST

Write the money amounts. Subtract.

100¢
− 45¢
55¢

69¢
− 21¢
48¢

Solve the problems.

The bulletin board is 122 centimeters long.

The paper is 150 centimeters long.

How much paper should be cut off to fit the board?
__28__ cm

Thomas has 5 dimes, 1 nickel, and 8 pennies.

He wants to buy a postcard for 55¢

Does he have enough money? __yes__

Spectrum Subtraction
Grade 2

Check What You Learned
Chapter 5
71

Final Test Chapters 1–5

Subtract.

79	7	18	43	12	68
− 43	− 2	− 9	− 15	− 3	− 15
36	5	9	28	9	53

30	15	10	46	3	43
− 19	− 8	− 3	− 36	− 0	− 6
11	7	7	10	3	37

14	8	56	72	17	9
− 6	− 8	− 44	− 35	− 9	− 4
8	0	12	37	8	5

79	15	75	7	68	17
− 36	− 9	− 36	− 7	− 22	− 8
43	6	39	0	46	9

11	82	4	50	9	78
− 3	− 79	− 3	− 23	− 5	− 55
8	3	1	27	4	23

52	19	99	20	61	80
− 21	− 5	− 20	− 7	− 40	− 9
31	14	79	13	21	71

CHAPTERS 1–5 FINAL TEST

Spectrum Subtraction
Grade 2
72

Final Test
Chapters 1–5

Spectrum Subtraction
Grade 2

Answer Key

Final Test Chapters 1–5

Solve each problem.

Jenny is reading a book that is 98 pages long.
She has read 47 pages so far.
How many pages does Jenny have left to read? __51__
47 + __51__ = 98

Addison bakes 14 loaves of bread.
After she gives some away, she has 6 left.
How many loaves of bread did Addison give away? __8__
14 – __8__ = 6

Courtney had some fabric.
Becca gave her 12 more feet of fabric.
Now, Courtney has 65 feet of fabric.
How many feet of fabric did Courtney have to start with? __53__
__53__ + 12 = 65

There are 12 campers in the lake for an afternoon swim.
6 more campers join them.
If 9 of the campers get out of the lake,
how many campers are left swimming in the lake? __9__

Kayla raked leaves in her front yard for 55 minutes.
She raked leaves in her backyard for 26 minutes.
How much longer did Kayla spend raking in her front yard?
__29__ minutes

Final Test Chapters 1–5

Write the number shown by the blocks. Then, use the blocks to help you solve the subtraction problems.

 = __674__

674 – 200 = __474__   674 – 374 = __300__
674 – 400 = __274__   674 – 174 = __500__
674 – 600 = __74__   674 – 74 = __600__

= __328__

328 – 100 = __228__   328 – 228 = __100__
328 – 200 = __128__   328 – 128 = __200__
328 – 300 = __28__   328 – 28 = __300__

Count backward by tens.
890, 880, __870__, __860__, 850, __840__, __830__, 820, __810__

Count backward by hundreds.
862, __762__, 662, __562__, __462__, 362, __262__, __162__, 62

Write the number that is 10 less.
781 __771__   85 __75__   328 __318__

Write the number that is 100 less.
528 __428__   154 __54__   350 __250__

Final Test Chapters 1–5

Subtract.

881	803	746	202	236	318
– 17	– 29	– 48	– 96	– 48	– 45
864	774	698	106	188	273

802	438	877	602	930	738
– 359	– 118	– 335	– 420	– 115	– 309
443	320	542	182	815	429

118	813	946	145	918	226
– 71	– 320	– 439	– 91	– 110	– 14
47	493	507	54	808	212

925	408	770	789	967	571
– 666	– 121	– 162	– 601	– 18	– 101
259	287	608	188	949	470

Write the same number to complete each pair of equations.

[64] – 17 47	47 + 17 [64]	308 – [263] 45	45 + [263] 308	51 – 47 [4]	[4] + 47 51
[478] – 59 419	419 + 59 [478]	337 – [105] 232	232 + [105] 337	[18] – 18 0	0 + 18 [18]

Final Test Chapters 1–5

Measure each object. Tell how much longer one object is than the other.

__2__ cm   __5__ cm

__3__ cm longer

Write the money amounts. Subtract.

80¢

– 73 ¢
7 ¢

Solve the problems.

Mr. Shaw bought 27 yards of fabric to make curtains.
Ms. Wolf bought 36 yards of fabric to make curtains.
How much more fabric did Ms. Wolf buy? __9__ yards

A cone of popcorn cost 69¢.
Mia paid with 3 quarters.
How much change did Mia receive? __6__ ¢

Blake earned 90¢ for taking out the trash.
He lent 25¢ to his little sister.
How much did Blake have left? __65__ ¢

Spectrum Subtraction
Grade 2

Answer Key

Notes